THE CURE FOR DEATH BY LIGHTNING

the Cure for Death by Lightning

A play adapted by
DARYL CLORAN
from the novel by
GAIL ANDERSON-DARGATZ

Talonbooks

Talonbooks
278 East First Avenue, Vancouver, British Columbia, Canada v5T 1A6
www.talonbooks.com

First printing: 2018

Typeset in Tribute
Printed and bound in Canada on 100% post-consumer recycled paper

Cover photograph by Barbara Zimonick
Cover and interior design by Chloë Filson

Talonbooks acknowledges the financial support of the Canada Council for the Arts, the Government of Canada through the Canada Book Fund, and the Province of British Columbia through the British Columbia Arts Council and the Book Publishing Tax Credit.

LIBRARY AND ARCHIVES CANADA CATALOGUING IN PUBLICATION

Cloran, Daryl, author
  The cure for death by lightning / a play adapted by Daryl
Cloran from the novel by Gail Anderson-Dargatz ; with a foreword
by Gail Anderson-Dargatz.

ISBN 978-1-77201-205-7 (softcover)

  I. Title. II. Anderson-Dargatz, Gail, 1963– . Cure for death by lightning

PS8605.L65C87 2018   C812'.6   C2018-901030-4

CONTENTS

FOREWORD

On a late October day in 2013, Daryl Cloran met with me at a small café opposite the Kamloops Art Gallery. He wanted to get my input as he wrote his stage adaptation of my novel *The Cure for Death by Lightning*. More to the point, he was there to assure me that I could see the work at each stage of its development and make sure I approved.

I think I surprised Daryl when I told him the story was his baby now and all I wanted were two tickets to opening night; I would keep my hands out of the process. Most writers want a say in how their novels are adapted, and I sure understand why. But I trusted Daryl's vision. I knew he would carry the essence of the novel forward in a way that was appropriate for the stage. And he did, brilliantly. You see the evidence here in your hands.

For me, stepping back from Daryl's project was all about passing the story on, because this really wasn't my story in the first place. The novel was inspired, in large part, by the tales my mother told me about her life as a teen during the Second World War. She was struck by lightning. She saw flowers rain down from the sky. She was chased by ghosts and, in the woods, by ... something. That's not to say that Beth, the main character in *The Cure for Death by Lightning*, is my mother. She's not. But the story was woven from threads of stories my mother told.

In 2017, the first stage production of *The Cure for Death by Lightning* was mounted, appropriately, in Kamloops – in the landscape of the novel, the Shuswap and Thompson-Okanagan regions. Daryl directed the play, and he and everyone involved in the production put heart and soul into it. Sitting in the audience on opening night, I had the uncanny sense that I was viewing one of my own dreams from the outside. More than that, I felt the profound presence of my mother, Irene Anderson, in that auditorium, though she had passed away a decade before. She had told me her stories. I had taken those stories and written my own. In turn, Daryl had taken the story and transformed it yet again, into this magical vision that played out on the stage. It was now a story passed from hand to hand and reshaped along the way. But of course, that's all storytellers – *all* of us – ever do: we act as conduits for narratives passed from one generation to the next, each generation adding something to the story or transforming it in some way.

So, here's to you, Daryl, for picking up the thread and carrying the story forward. You've taken my dream, spun from my mother's experiences, and brought it vividly to life in a wholly new form, in a way I never could have imagined. For that, and the loving care you took with the story, I will be forever grateful.

—GAIL ANDERSON-DARGATZ
January 2018

PREFACE

When I became the Artistic Director of Western Canada Theatre (WCT) in 2010, one of the first things I did was start reading novels set in this region. I wanted to find a great Kamloops story I could adapt for the stage. When I picked up *The Cure for Death by Lightning* by Gail Anderson-Dargatz, I couldn't put it down. Gail has created such compelling characters and such a moving story, but more than that, she has created a story in which the land itself is a major character. The play is set just down the road from Kamloops in Turtle Valley, and the trees, the grass, the animals, the seasons, all play an enormous, important role in Anderson-Dargatz's storytelling. I was immediately struck by the evocative images Gail had created and the inherent theatricality of the story; it seemed so perfect for the stage. So I decided to give it a try.

Gail has been incredibly supportive of this adaptation every step of the way. When I first met with her to pitch the idea, I promised to bring her each new draft of the script to approve. She smiled and said, "Just give me tickets to opening night." It is such a generous (and courageous) act to trust your characters and story to another artist adapting it to another medium. Now, over a few years and a few drafts, this stage adaptation has emerged, one that is intended to honour Gail's heart-wrenching story while transforming itself to embrace the strengths of theatrical storytelling.

At its core, the story is about the relationship between Canada's settlers and Indigenous people, and our shared connection to the land – all seen from the unique perspective of a fifteen-year-old girl. The script and production have benefitted immensely from consultation with great Indigenous theatre artists like Kevin Loring, Kim Harvey, Jeff Chief, and WCT's own Lori Marchand.

The Cure for Death by Lightning was the final show I directed during my tenure as Artistic Director of WCT. Staging this play, based on a local novel, was the perfect way to say thank you and farewell to a theatre and a city that had welcomed me so openly. I am a better artist and, I dare say, a better human being, thanks to the six years I spent in this incredible region.

—DARYL CLORAN
June 2017

THE CURE FOR
DEATH BY LIGHTNING

PRODUCTION HISTORY

The Cure for Death by Lightning was first produced by Western Canada Theatre from April 6 to 15, 2017, at the Sagebrush Theatre in Kamloops, British Columbia, with the following cast and crew:

BETH: Lucy Hill
MOTHER: Anita Wittenberg
FATHER: Andrew Wheeler
DENNIS: Taran Kootenhayoo
FILTHY BILLY: Aaron M. Wells
NORA: Joelle Peters
CRAZY JACK: Braden Griffiths

Director: Daryl Cloran
Set and Props Designer: Marshall McMahen
Costume Designer: Marian Truscott
Lighting Designer: Gerald King
Composer and Sound Designer: John Gzowski
Puppet Design and Construction: Braden Griffiths
Cultural Consultant and Assistant Director: Kim Harvey
Assistant Director: Andrew G. Cooper
Fight Director: Karl Sine
Dramaturge: Kevin Loring
Design Consultant: Jeff Chief
Stage Manager: Lisa Russell
Assistant Stage Manager: Christine Leroux
Apprentice Stage Manager: Leigh Robinson

PRODUCTION NOTE

The animals are represented by large-scale puppets. The puppets are not meant to be realistic; instead they should be representative and emerge magically from the environment of the play. For example, the bear could rise out of a dirt mound on the stage, and the birds could be articles of laundry hanging on a line that suddenly fly across the yard. While the animals should be life-sized, they do not need to be fully articulated and lifelike. Each serves a storytelling purpose, and those purposes should figure prominently in the design. For example, the bear represents great threat and physical danger, thus its jaws and claws are the key elements.

This story should be propelled by simple, physical, theatrical magic. Crazy Jack (with the help of the rest of the ensemble) manipulates the animal puppets and creates the physical transformations and magic of the show. For example, the swathes that are cut through the tall grass can be made by Crazy Jack, and he can pull the hundreds of turtles across Blood Road.

The story takes place in numerous locations and moves quickly, so the settings should appear and disappear as needed. Sets shouldn't be overly literal, and the play shouldn't depend on complicated set changes. As with the puppets, I encourage anyone mounting this play to use only what is needed. For instance, the audience only needs to see the portions of the house that are necessary in each particular scene. In the original production, sometimes only the kitchen was seen, sometimes both the kitchen and living room, and sometimes the kitchen, living room, and Beth's bedroom all at once.

Filthy Billy's outbursts are notated in parentheses within his lines of dialogue. These indications are guidelines; there is room for the actor to personalize Billy's language (and use more than just the two words indicated).

....

CHARACTERS

BETH Weeks, fifteen years old

MOTHER of Beth, in her forties

John Weeks, FATHER of Beth; in his forties; a big, strong man and a farmer

DENNIS, eighteen; Indigenous; cousin to Billy and Nora; works as a hired hand on the Weeks's farm

FILTHY BILLY, nineteen; Indigenous; cousin to Dennis and Nora; works as a hired hand on the Weeks's farm; suffers from Tourette's syndrome

NORA, fifteen; cousin to Billy and Dennis; mixed parentage (Indigenous mother, settler father)

CRAZY JACK Johannsen, the Swede's son; in his twenties; lives in the bush, haunted, isolated

ANIMALS

The following animals appear in the story. They may be represented on stage by life-sized puppets and in other ways as described here.

BEAR, which should emerge from the ground. A head with jaws, and it needs paws/claws for batting at sheep and Father

SHEEP, seen in the shadows on the plateau. Perhaps the sheep are white tumbleweeds with heads

DOGS, audio only. Not seen on stage

BIRDS, which are also articles of laundry hanging on a clothesline

CHERRY, the family horse that pulls the democrat wagon

LUCIFER, a black cat that walks in circles

Brindled COW that Father kills with a sledgehammer to the head. The head is the important part – it needs to be crushed by the impact of the sledgehammer

Hundreds of TURTLES must appear to cross the stage

FAWN, a young deer that appears in the bush. Perhaps it is built out of branches

ACT 1

....

SCENE 1

Darkness. From the distance, the ferocious growl of a BEAR.

Adams Plateau, British Columbia.

Inside a canvas tent, a lantern is lit. Three shadows can be seen inside: MOTHER, FATHER, and BETH. It is night. Outside the tent, only the moon illuminates the surroundings. Around the tent, SHEEP bleat fearfully.

FATHER emerges from the tent, holding a rifle. All is silent. He waits. BETH emerges from the tent, holding a small rifle. They speak in whispers.

FATHER
  Get back in the tent.

BETH
  I want to help.

MOTHER emerges from the tent.

FATHER
Both of you, go back. It's not safe.

MOTHER
No.

> *FATHER looks in exasperation at MOTHER and BETH but realizes there's no reasoning with them on this.*

FATHER
(*relenting*) Fine. But stay here.

BETH
The sheep are upset.

FATHER
I know.

> *FATHER explores, moving farther away from the tent, gun ready. MOTHER and BETH wait anxiously.*

> *Nothing.*

FATHER
(*turning back to MOTHER and BETH*) It's okay, there's noth–

> *Suddenly, from amidst the SHEEP, an enormous grizzly BEAR rises up on its hind legs, roaring and swatting. The silence of the night is split by the deafening roar of the BEAR and the barks of DOGS (sheepdogs). Pandemonium. SHEEP scatter in all directions.*

> *FATHER fires his rifle. He misses. The BEAR starts to charge at the family.*

FATHER

Oh Jesus. Get down! Get down!

> *FATHER and MOTHER drop to the ground. BETH panics.*
> *She runs for the tent with the BEAR chasing her. She trips*
> *and falls.*

> *BETH fires her little rifle at the BEAR. The BEAR howls and*
> *runs off into the bush, pursued by the barking DOGS.*

> *FATHER rushes to BETH. He falls to his knees beside her*
> *and shakes her.*

FATHER

Are you all right? Are you all right?

BETH

I got him.

FATHER

Sure, you got him. (*to MOTHER*) Stay with her.

> *FATHER cocks his gun and marches into the bush after the*
> *BEAR. Everyone waits.*

BETH

I got it. I know I did.

MOTHER

Enough. Stay sharp.

> *A gunshot. Everyone's attention snaps to the spot where*
> *FATHER entered the bush. Silence.*

> *Finally, FATHER returns. He walks to MOTHER. She lifts*
> *the lantern to his face. He is shaking and covered in bits of*

undergrowth, with claw-like scratches on each side of his
face. His eyes look wild.

MOTHER
John, what happened?

FATHER doesn't answer. He stumbles toward the tent.

MOTHER
Did you get him?

Finally, FATHER answers.

FATHER
I don't know ... so dark. Something came after me. I shot
it ... I think I shot it ...

MOTHER helps FATHER into the tent. BETH looks to the
audience.

BETH
(*to the audience*) We watched for the grizzly all night, but he
didn't return. We had spent that whole summer sleeping in
a tent, herding our sheep from one grazing area to the next.
But the bear attack put an end to all the glorious summers we
spent wandering the mountains.

The set changes behind BETH; the plateau disappears and
the farmhouse is assembled.

BETH
My name is Beth Weeks. My story takes place in the midst of
the Second World War, the year I turned fifteen, the year the
world fell apart and began to come together again.

·················

SCENE 2

Summer.

BETH stands in front of the farmhouse. Laundry hangs on a line.

The deafening chatter of BIRDS. Suddenly the articles of laundry leap from the line and fly into the air, and the sky over the farm is aflutter with (laundry) BIRDS.

BETH watches them fly overhead, then notices FATHER and MOTHER approaching the farm, riding in their democrat wagon, pulled by the family horse, CHERRY.

BETH
You're home! (*running to the democrat*) How was Kamloops? Good day? Did you buy me anything?

FATHER just grunts and unloads provisions from the democrat into the house.

MOTHER reaches into her pocket and pulls out a small square of chocolate wrapped in foil. She hands it to BETH.

MOTHER
Here. Don't tell your father.

BETH
Thank you!

BETH hugs MOTHER and gobbles up the chocolate.

BETH

What did the doctor in town say about Dad?

MOTHER

He says maybe his blood's weak. That's why he eats so much. I don't think he's anemic. That would make him tired. He doesn't sleep anymore. And for all the food he eats, he doesn't gain weight.

BETH

Did he say why Dad's grumpy all the time?

MOTHER shakes her head.

BETH

I miss the old Dad.

MOTHER

He brought home a porcupine last week. He skinned it and cleaned it and said, "It's chicken." I said, "That's not chicken." He said, "I say it's chicken, so it's chicken." So I cooked it as if it were chicken.

BETH

I knew that wasn't chicken! It was awful.

MOTHER and BETH laugh. Suddenly the screen door bangs shut and FATHER is standing with them on the porch.

FATHER

What are you laughing at?

MOTHER and BETH regain their composure.

MOTHER

Nothing. Just good to be home.

MOTHER reaches to touch FATHER's face gently, but he pushes her hand away and stalks off toward the democrat. FATHER walks past a bird pecking at seed in the yard. He kicks at it. The bird squawks in alarm and flies away. BETH and MOTHER make eye contact, concerned about FATHER.

MOTHER

(*to BETH*) Start serving dinner. I'll wash up.

BETH heads inside to the kitchen. She busies herself by preparing dinner, pulling the chicken out of the oven.

DENNIS and FILTHY BILLY enter from the yard.

DENNIS

Chicken again tonight? That was good chicken we had last week, eh, Filthy Billy?

DENNIS winks at BETH.

FILTHY BILLY

(Shit) I took some of them (fuck) chicken quills home for (shit) Granny's moccasins.

DENNIS leans against the cupboard beside BETH.

DENNIS

You going to be my girlfriend?

BETH enjoys the proximity for a moment, but then looks past DENNIS, toward the yard.

BETH

He's just out there.

*BETH goes back to work on the chicken. DENNIS takes
BETH's hand.*

DENNIS

I think you want to be my girlfriend.

BETH

I think you got hands like sandpaper.

> *FILTHY BILLY laughs. FATHER enters. FILTHY BILLY
> attempts to contain his laughter. DENNIS moves away from
> BETH, but not before FATHER notes how close the two were.
> MOTHER enters from the hall. The kitchen is bustling now;
> everyone taking their places at the table for dinner.*

FATHER

Goddamned Swede took down part of our fence again. You
see that? We'll fix him. Tonight, you hear?

> *MOTHER looks upset about this. She attempts to change
> the subject.*

MOTHER

(*to BETH*) Is your dress clean for the funeral?

BETH

Yes.

MOTHER

You should set your hair tonight. (*to DENNIS*) You going to
Sarah Kemp's funeral tomorrow?

DENNIS

(*shaking his head*) Didn't know her.

MOTHER

I guess the whole town will be going. Mauled by some
animal – it's no way for a little girl to die. Bet it was the
same grizzly that attacked our camp last month. That could
have been you, Beth, if that grizzly reached you ... We were
so lucky.

DENNIS

I heard she was all ripped apart. Her stomach all eaten up.

MOTHER

Enough.

BETH puts her fork down and pushes her plate away.

DENNIS

I killed a bear with a .22 once. The trick is to get real close,
then throw your arms up, like you're challenging the bear.
When the bear stands up, on its hind legs, and growls at
you, when its mouth is open, that's when you shoot it,
through the mouth!

FATHER

What a bunch of baloney.

DENNIS

That's an old Indian way. Taught to me by my grandfather.

FATHER

That's bullshit!

MOTHER

Enough!

DENNIS

(*grinning*) Yeah, well, it's a good story anyway.

FILTHY BILLY

That (fuck) wasn't no animal. (Shit.) Bears don't attack like that.

MOTHER

It must have gone rabid.

FILTHY BILLY

It was (fuck) Crazy Jack.

MOTHER

No man's capable of that.

BETH

The Swede's son?

FILTHY BILLY

Coyote's come and took him over.

MOTHER

Hush. Just because he lives alone ...

FILTHY BILLY

A man stays out in the bush alone long enough (fuck), the bush changes him.

BETH listens, wide-eyed.

DENNIS

(*to get a rise out of BETH*) They say she was pulled apart from the crotch up. And the tops of her legs were just gone. What do you think Crazy Jack did with her legs?

MOTHER

You should be ashamed of yourself, talking that way about your neighbour.

FATHER

The Swede's crazy enough. Wouldn't be surprised if his kid was too.

MOTHER

John!

They continue dinner in silence.

DENNIS

(*to MOTHER*) Granny wants to know if she can buy a little cream from you?

MOTHER

You know I can't sell it off the farm, with the rationing.

DENNIS

(*clawing at the air*) I thought maybe a bear could come raid your can, eh?

FATHER

Go ahead.

Everyone looks to him, surprised.

DENNIS

Well seein' as you're in a charitable mood, how 'bout a raise?

The flash of kindness quickly disappears from FATHER.

FATHER

You've barely been here two months.

DENNIS

Lots of guys on the reserve have gone off and joined up. Soon there won't be nobody left to work on the farms.

FATHER

You're not going to enlist; we both know that.

DENNIS

If me and Filthy Billy don't get paid like we should, maybe we will.

> *FATHER's face goes red, and he clenches and unclenches his fists.*

> *Throughout this exchange, FILTHY BILLY has been attempting to hold in an inevitable explosion of cursing. Finally, he can't help himself. He jumps up, grabs the leg bone off the chicken and a couple of buns, and runs out the door, knocking over his chair on the way.*

FATHER

(*yelling after FILTHY BILLY*) Pick that up!

> *But FILTHY BILLY is already in the backyard, off stage, letting out the string of curse words that had been building up inside him.*

FATHER

(*muttering to himself*) Filthy idiot.

> *DENNIS stands, picks up BILLY's chair, and sets it right. He lingers near BETH and gives her a knowing glance.*

DENNIS

Good chicken. Almost as good as last week's.

> *DENNIS laughs. FATHER looks at him, then storms out of the room.*

MOTHER

He gets angry and it washes away. It'll be all right ...

DENNIS

(*lowering his voice*) He's not right in the head anymore. You be careful. You and Beth.

> *DENNIS winks at BETH and then heads out to the field to work, leaving BETH and MOTHER in the kitchen. The sound of Enrico Caruso drifts in from the living room. MOTHER turns to the sink to start washing dishes.*

MOTHER

(*Dismissing Dennis's warning*) He'll be fine.

> *BETH walks into the living room. She sees FATHER sitting in his armchair, listening to Enrico Caruso on the gramophone. FATHER tears up, wipes his eyes, and looks away from her. BETH considers Dennis's warning.*

SCENE 3

Later that evening. BETH sits on a hollow tree stump near Turtle Creek. This is her safe space. She reaches deep into the stump and pulls out a small bundle wrapped in red velvet. She opens the velvet to reveal a tube of lipstick and a bottle of perfume. BETH brushes the scrap of velvet against her face and her neck, luxuriating in its softness. Then she reaches down under her skirt and rubs the velvet against her inner thigh sensually. She opens the bottle of perfume and smells it. She dabs some perfume on her wrist. She breathes deeply. She holds her wrist forward for an imaginary suitor to inhale.

BETH
What is that captivating scent, you ask? (*coyly*) A woman must have her secrets.

She rolls up her sleeve and puts some lipstick in the crook of her arm. BETH continues play-acting with her imaginary suitor.

No, Dennis, I can't. All right, just one more kiss. But we've gotta be careful.

BETH leans in and kisses the crook of her arm.

No, no, that's all. For now. Now wipe away the lipstick or everyone will know.

BETH wipes the lipstick away, lost in her imaginary romance. After a moment, she stops, suspicious. Looking around, she discovers a young girl – NORA – in the trees,

watching her. NORA wears a necklace of small bells. BETH
and NORA make eye contact.

BETH
Who are you?

> *NORA suddenly disappears into the trees, her bells making a*
> *quiet jingling sound.*

BETH
(*yelling after NORA*) Hey!

> *But NORA is gone. BETH bundles her illicit treasures back*
> *into the velvet and tucks them away. She hears a sudden*
> *noise – like something is cutting a path through the field*
> *straight at her. She freezes. The noise is getting closer.*
> *BETH backs up, but the noise keeps coming. She turns and*
> *runs toward the hired hands' cabin. The thing in the grass*
> *is almost on top of her now. She reaches the cabin door and*
> *bangs furiously.*

> *The door opens. It's DENNIS. The noise stops.*

DENNIS
Well my girlfriend's here!

> *BETH looks frantically behind her but can find nothing. The*
> *evening is silent.*

DENNIS
You okay?

BETH
Yeah. Fine.

BETH notices DENNIS is shirtless. She becomes embarrassed and tries not to stare. FILTHY BILLY emerges from the cabin and sits by the fire. He begins tying a length of binder twine around his pant leg.

BETH

What's he doing?

DENNIS

He saw a black lizard today. You know those little guys, about this long. (*indicating three inches*) That's so the lizard doesn't get up his pants and eat his heart.

BETH

I see those lizards all the time. Never ate my heart.

DENNIS

I guess they don't like white meat.

FILTHY BILLY wheezes out a laugh.

BETH

If he's so worried about his heart, why doesn't he tie his shirtsleeves shut?

DENNIS

The lizard enters your body someplace lower.

DENNIS grins wickedly at BETH. She immediately grows shy.

DENNIS

He's going to jump over the fire. So the lizard'll get burnt up. Anyway, did you want something?

DENNIS moves closer to BETH. BETH looks at her feet and shakes her head. FILTHY BILLY heads back into the cabin.

DENNIS
Just come for a visit, eh? (*touching her face*) You just come over anytime.

DENNIS enters the cabin and shuts the door. BETH lingers by the campfire, wary of heading back into the darkening night. She hears meowing. She almost trips over a black cat walking circles in front of her. BETH picks up the cat and strokes it.

BETH
Hey, little guy. Who are you? Be careful; father doesn't take kindly to animals anymore.

Suddenly, a voice from the field.

FATHER
Beth!

BETH panics. She searches for a place to hide. She tucks the cat into her coat. Suddenly a hand grabs her and slams her up against the wall of the cabin. It's FATHER.

FATHER
Don't you ever come to this cabin. Hear me? You hear me?

A long, tense silence, broken by the sound of mewing. FATHER looks down at BETH's coat.

FATHER
What have you got there?

BETH
Nothing.

FATHER
Let's see.

> *Reluctantly, BETH opens her coat and reveals the cat to FATHER.*

FATHER
(*taking the cat*) Look at him!

BETH
Don't kill him, please.

FATHER
(*petting the cat*) Why would I kill him? Black cat. Satan's cat. Call him Lucifer. Take him to show Mother.

> *FILTHY BILLY emerges from the cabin.*

FILTHY BILLY
Did you see (fuck) the Swede has put his fence back up?

FATHER
That son of a bitch. I'll show him.

> *FATHER hands the cat back to BETH and runs to the house. BETH catches her breath, rattled from the encounter with her father. She puts the cat down. It resumes its circuit.*

FILTHY BILLY
You okay?

> *BETH shrugs. FILTHY BILLY looks to where FATHER left and then looks down at the cat, which is turning circles.*

FILTHY BILLY
He (fuck) keeps doing the same circles. Something's
haunting him.

BETH
He's probably just had a stroke.

> *They watch as the cat carves out the same circles again and
> again without varying.*

FILTHY BILLY
I should do him in.

BETH
Maybe leave him. Maybe he'll get better.

FILTHY BILLY
(Shit) Maybe.

> *They watch the cat walk in circles for another moment.*

BETH
Do you really think Crazy Jack Johannsen killed Sarah
Kemp?

FILTHY BILLY
He had Coyote in him. (Fuck) Coyote takes somebody (shit)
over, see? Possess him. (shit, fuck) You gotta stay away
from Coyote.

BETH
Coyote's a bad spirit?

FILTHY BILLY
Nah, not bad. No good guys and bad guys. (Fuck) The world
doesn't work like that. But if a man's got something wrong

with him, if he's a drunk (shit) or got hit on the head or something, then Coyote can get inside him like (shit) putting on a coat. While he's in there, there's no telling (fuck) what he'll do.

Silence. BETH takes this in.

FILTHY BILLY
Beautiful night, eh? (Shit). Excuse me. Sorry (fuck).

FILTHY BILLY scratches at the skin on his forearm.

BETH
Why do you scratch so much?

FILTHY BILLY
Sorry. I can't (fuck) help it. Excuse me. (Shit) You should go. Your dad's (shit) going to be mad. (Fuck, shit) Excuse me. (Shit) Sorry. (Fuck). You should go.

FILTHY BILLY begins to jump back and forth over the fire. BETH watches him for a moment, then looks down to the cat.

BETH
(*to the cat*) Come on, Lucifer.

BETH picks up the cat and heads back toward the house. After a few moments of walking, BETH feels a presence. CRAZY JACK emerges from the trees, watching her. He's gaunt and ragged, with a haunted, isolated look in his eyes. He holds flowers he has picked from the bush. BETH and CRAZY JACK make eye contact.

BETH

(*under her breath, to LUCIFER*) Crazy Jack. (*to CRAZY JACK, as if speaking cautiously to a young child*) Hi. Jack. Are you here because my dad's tearing down the fence again?

CRAZY JACK doesn't respond. He continues watching BETH.

BETH

Those are nice flowers. Who are they for? Are they for me?

BETH slowly approaches CRAZY JACK. He disappears into the trees, offstage. BETH watches for a moment to see if he'll return. Unsettled, BETH shivers.

BETH

(*to LUCIFER*) I wonder what he wants.

. . . .

SCENE 4

BETH runs in to the kitchen from outside. She holds LUCIFER inside her coat. She stands quietly in the corner and watches MOTHER, who is in her nightgown, as she attempts to talk sense into FATHER. FATHER is storming around, gathering supplies.

Mother's scrapbook lies open on the table.

MOTHER

At least talk to the man. You haven't talked to the man. Maybe he'll sell the land. Look at you! Building fences in the middle of the night!

FATHER puts on his boots.

MOTHER
Don't do this, please. You haven't even talked to him about it.
Just talk to him.

FATHER grabs a lantern.

MOTHER
Let me talk to him. It's all a mistake, I'm sure of it.

FATHER takes a gun from the gun rack.

MOTHER
You don't need a gun. Why are you taking a gun?

*MOTHER attempts to physically block the door, but FATHER
pushes past her and exits.*

MOTHER
(*calling after him*) He's got every right to shoot you! Every
right! (*banging around the kitchen angrily*) He hasn't got the
sense God gave a goose. (*continuing to mutter to herself*) Hell to
pay ... fool ... wasn't I right? (*looking up briefly, as if listening
to someone else talking*) No, no, I can't do that.

BETH moves closer to her mother.

BETH
Who are you talking to?

MOTHER turns, surprised to see BETH in the kitchen.

MOTHER
Oh ... Oh well, that's my mother.

BETH

What do you tell her?

MOTHER

Things. About the day.

BETH

Does she answer?

MOTHER

Oh, well, if I said yes, you'd think me crazy.

BETH

No, not crazy.

MOTHER

I think she's here with us. Sometimes I think that. (*noticing LUCIFER*) What do we have here?

BETH

Father says I can keep him. He named him Lucifer.

MOTHER

Well there's no telling. He always had a soft spot for animals. Maybe your father is coming back to his old self. (*flipping through her scrapbook, looking for something*) I had a clipping in here about ... (*finding it*) Ah, there it is! (*reading*) Butter. (*taking the cat from BETH and applying some butter to each of its paws*) This will keep him home. He won't wander. (*pause*) I should put butter on *your* paws. I worry when you're out in the bush. It's not safe out there. A coyote killed another one of our sheep last night.

BETH

I take a gun.

BETH absent-mindedly flips open the scrapbook.

MOTHER
Leave it!

BETH
Okay.

MOTHER
How many times do I need to tell you to leave my scrapbook alone!

BETH
(*slamming the scrapbook shut*) Okay!

Beat.

MOTHER
I didn't mean to snap.

*MOTHER turns back to her work in the kitchen and begins
to mutter, again, to her dead mother.*

. . . .

SCENE 5

*Daytime. BETH and DENNIS walk through the field.
DENNIS carries a shotgun, and BETH her small rifle.*

BETH
Where are you going in the evenings? You got some girl?

DENNIS

(*laughing*) Jealous?

BETH

(*embarrassed*) No.

DENNIS

No girls. Just trapping. I set some snares. Caught a coyote the other night. Trying to stop them from eating all your dad's sheep. (*pause*) Just gotta get out of here, you know?

BETH

I know. (*pause*) That was some funeral. So many people. Felt like the whole town was there.

DENNIS

Everyone's scared it's going to happen to their kid too.

> *They reach a clearing. DENNIS sets up three tin cans on a tree stump for target practice.*

BETH

I saw Crazy Jack. He's been hanging around the house. Looking like he wants to come in for a visit.

DENNIS

A visit? Ha!

BETH

I saw him last night. He had flowers. And then today at the funeral I saw him in town. He put the flowers on Sarah Kemp's grave. (*pause*) You ever see anything weird? Something following you?

DENNIS

Why, what'd you see?

BETH

I don't know. Something. Most of the time, I think I'm
imagining it.

DENNIS

You take that gun with you when you go out?

BETH

Sometimes.

DENNIS shoots a tin can, knocking it over.

DENNIS

Take it all the time. Crazy Jack is trouble.

BETH

Billy says Jack's got Coyote in him.

DENNIS

(*laughing*) Billy loves his Coyote stories. He'll tell them to
anyone that'll listen. Only way he can make sense of his dad
killing himself. That Kemp girl was killed by a man, not
a spirit.

BETH

Do you think it was Jack?

DENNIS

Maybe. Maybe someone else.

BETH

Who else?

DENNIS

There's lots of people who ain't right in the head around
here. Just take the gun.

BETH
Okay.

DENNIS shoots another tin can, knocking it over too.

DENNIS
Your turn.

BETH fires once and misses. She fires a second time and hits the can. They walk to the cans and set them upright again.

DENNIS
Filthy Billy is sweet on you. He took the job this summer because of you.

BETH
(slapping him on the shoulder) Filthy Billy!

DENNIS
What? You don't want to go out with Filthy Billy? You'd make a sweet couple.

BETH slaps him again. DENNIS laughs. Then BETH turns and pops off the tin can targets, one after the other, without missing.

DENNIS
You're getting to be a good shot.

BETH
You really going to enlist?

DENNIS
Better than staying here.

BETH

I don't want you to go.

DENNIS

I'd stay if you were my girlfriend.

> *DENNIS wraps his arms around BETH. He slides his hands down Beth's arms and puts his face in her hair. BETH lingers for a moment but then pulls away.*

DENNIS

Can't leave you with your dad. He's crazy. You've got to think about leaving, yourself. Find someplace to go. There's lots of jobs now, in Vancouver, Calgary. They say all a girl's got to do is walk up to the factory door and she's got a job.

> *BETH shrugs. Somewhere in the distance, a coyote howls.*

DENNIS

You know what Filthy Billy says? He says a coyote howling sounds like a whole bunch of them howling because a coyote howls from both ends.

> *DENNIS farts. BETH laughs. Suddenly, a loud crack of thunder. DENNIS looks up at the sky.*

DENNIS

You head back. I'll get the cows in.

> *DENNIS leaves. BETH sees something in the woods. It's NORA. NORA watches BETH with interest.*

BETH

Hi.

NORA disappears into the woods, offstage, her necklace of bells jingling.

BETH
Wait! Come back!

BETH is about to pursue, but the sky opens up and rain starts to pelt down. BETH runs for home.

. . . .

SCENE 6

BETH enters the kitchen from outside. She takes off her wet coat. FATHER enters from outside. An uncomfortable beat.

FATHER
Where's your mother?

BETH
I don't know. The barn, likely.

FATHER
Dennis?

BETH
Bringing in the cows.

FATHER takes a long drink of water. He stares at BETH.

FATHER
You're all wet. Go to your room.

BETH

Why?

FATHER

Go to your room.

BETH

I don't want –

FATHER

Go to your room!

>*FATHER throws his empty cup across the room. It slams into the wall and clatters to the ground. BETH walks to her bedroom. FATHER moves to stand in her doorway.*

FATHER

Lay on the bed. Pull up your dress.

BETH

Why? What do you –

FATHER

Do it. Now.

>*BETH does as she's told. She lies on the bed and pulls up her dress. She squeezes her eyes closed, tense and scared, not sure what's about to happen.*

>*The front door slams shut as MOTHER enters the house. FATHER flinches. MOTHER sees FATHER standing at the door to Beth's room. MOTHER and FATHER make eye contact. MOTHER looks at BETH. BETH quickly pulls her dress down.*

MOTHER

Get cleaned up for supper.

> *BETH nods. MOTHER begins to work in the kitchen,*
> *avoiding looking at FATHER. FATHER exits to the yard.*

> *Outside, thunder cracks and the rain pours harder. BETH*
> *gets up from her bed and opens the window to watch the rain.*
> *Impulsively, she climbs out the window and stands in the*
> *rain, letting it pour down on her.*

> *The rain begins to transform. It looks purple. The raindrops*
> *seem to float. BETH holds her hand out to catch the drops.*
> *She realizes it's not rain.*

BETH

(*wonderously*) Violet flax.

> *The ground outside is now a carpet of purple flowers. BETH*
> *spins around in the growing piles of flax, inhaling the*
> *intoxicating smell. The flax continues to fall.*

> *BETH becomes aware of a sound behind her. She stops*
> *abruptly and listens: a swooshing sound, getting louder.*
> *Something is moving quickly toward BETH.*

> *Panicked, BETH begins to run for safety. She runs toward*
> *the fence. But now the sound is coming from that direction.*
> *BETH pivots, to escape in the opposite direction, and runs*
> *directly into NORA.*

NORA

Hi.

> *BETH looks back to the fence, but the sound is gone.*

NORA

What are you running from?

BETH

Nothing.

NORA

You okay?

BETH nods her head, still catching her breath.

BETH

Who are you?

NORA

Nora. Dennis's cousin. And Filthy Billy's.

BETH

I saw you. Watching me.

NORA nods, unapologetic.

NORA

Some storm, eh? Look at all those flowers! Ever seen anything so pretty?

NORA takes BETH's hand. BETH is surprised by this at first but quickly grows to like it, like a shared secret. Together they watch the last of the petals fall. Finally, BETH looks at NORA's bell necklace.

NORA

Like it? I made it.

NORA jingles the necklace for BETH. They both smile.
BETH looks from the necklace to NORA's arm, where there
are bloody cuts.

BETH
What happened to your arm?

NORA quickly rolls her sleeve down.

NORA
Nothing.

BETH
(reaching for NORA's arm) Let's see. You did that, didn't you?

NORA
So what if I did?

BETH
Doesn't it hurt?

NORA
Mind your own business. Dennis says your father's gone
stupid.

BETH flushes with anger but says nothing.

NORA
I'm sorry. Dennis says that about a lot of people.

BETH shrugs.

BETH
After that bear attacked our camp ... He hasn't been right.

NORA

Something got him, in the bush.

BETH

The bear.

NORA

No. Something's out there. Something you can't see. It got him and made him turn.

> BETH takes in NORA's warning. They stand in silence for a moment.

BETH

Are you from the reserve? Do you go to Indian school?

NORA

Nope. Don't go to school. I'm not a real Indian anyhow.

BETH

I hate school.

NORA

I guess I wouldn't mind going, but not to the residential school. They made my mother crazy. They beat my uncle. They wouldn't call him by his real name. They called him Samuel. What kind of place takes away your name?

> Beat.

> BETH gestures to rocks on the ground.

BETH

There're children buried under there.

NORA

I know it.

BETH

How do you know that?

NORA

Everyone knows that.

BETH

How did they die?

NORA

Killed by the same thing that killed Sarah Kemp.

BETH

But that was years ago.

> *NORA nods.*

BETH

I think I hear them sometimes. Knocking around.

NORA

They're trying to warn you.

BETH

That's silly.

> *BETH kicks the ground.*

NORA

I like your hair.

> *NORA reaches out and runs her fingers through BETH's hair for some time. BETH enjoys it.*

NORA

You're beautiful. Like an angel.

BETH turns to speak, but FATHER unexpectedly appears.

FATHER

(*to NORA*) You! Get away from here, you lousy Indian. Get off my property!

NORA turns and flees.

BETH

I'm sorry, I just climbed out my window to see the rain and …

BETH sees that FATHER is unsteady and crying.

BETH

You're cry– … Are you okay?

FATHER turns away from BETH. BETH interprets his tears as an apology for his recent behaviour.

BETH

It's okay, you didn't mean –

FATHER

That's our entire flax crop, ruined. The crops that feed the cows, feed us. What are we going to do?

FATHER turns and walks away, leaving BETH alone, stunned. Just then, she hears a sound. She listens, wondering: Were the rocks rattling?

SCENE 7

Autumn. BETH enters the barn. She gathers her milking bucket and stool. She wipes her face with her skirt, revealing her legs. DENNIS enters the barn and sees her.

DENNIS
Hey, nice legs!

BETH pushes her skirt down and looks around anxiously for FATHER.

DENNIS
He's out in the field.

DENNIS steps into the calf's stall where BETH is. She steps back against the wall. He moves toward her slowly. He puts his hands on her arms.

BETH
What if he sees?

DENNIS wraps his arms around BETH's waist and kisses her. BETH responds in kind.

FATHER enters the barn behind them.

FATHER
What the hell?

FATHER grabs DENNIS by the shoulders and pushes him against the wall.

FATHER

What the hell? (*pushing DENNIS into the wall again*) What the hell? (*and again*)

> *DENNIS struggles to get a hold of FATHER's arms and then pushes FATHER away. Hearing the commotion, FILTHY BILLY and MOTHER run into the barn. FILTHY BILLY steps between FATHER and DENNIS, prying them apart.*

MOTHER

Enough! Stop it!

FATHER

(*pointing at DENNIS*) You get out of here now! Take your things and get out!

MOTHER

We need him. We've got the corn to do.

FATHER

I won't have him here.

MOTHER

There's no harm done.

FATHER

Don't you ever come near my daughter again!

> *A tense standoff between FATHER and DENNIS is interrupted by a loud groan from a COW.*

FILTHY BILLY

That cow is dying.

FATHER

Give her time.

DENNIS
She's suffering. There's maggots in that wound you made.

FATHER
She'll heal up.

BETH
What happened?

DENNIS
He cut out her ovaries so she'd gain weight and he could sell her for more. Stupid idea.

FATHER
You shut your mouth.

DENNIS
If you're not going to, I'll kill her myself.

FATHER
Leave her.

FILTHY BILLY
(Shit) She's dying.

> *FILTHY BILLY is overcome by a wave of cursing so violent it takes the breath from him and makes him sit down. Everyone watches him, amazed.*

FATHER
I'll do it.

DENNIS
What?

FATHER
I said I'll do it, goddamn it.

DENNIS

> Then I'll help you.

FATHER

> I don't want your help. The girl.

MOTHER

> She'll be late for school.

FATHER

> Let her.

MOTHER

> Let Dennis help, for heaven's sake!

FATHER

> No! The girl. She needs to learn.

> *BETH looks to her mother for help.*

MOTHER

> (*to BETH*) Try not to be late. (*to DENNIS and FILTHY BILLY*) You two, come load the democrat. We're taking the cream to Kamloops today.

> *MOTHER, FILTHY BILLY, and DENNIS leave the barn. On his way out, DENNIS gives BETH a look of warning. FATHER prepares to kill the COW.*

FATHER

> Come over here.

> *BETH crosses to her father and the COW. The COW is lying on the ground, moaning, clearly in a lot of pain. FATHER motions for BETH to come hold the COW's rope halter.*

FATHER

Hold tight. Pull it so her head is flat on the floor.

> *BETH tugs on the rope, pulling the COW's head to the floor. FATHER grabs a sledgehammer that is lying against the wall. He lifts it high and brings it down directly onto the COW's forehead. BETH looks away. The COW jerks from the impact of the blow. FATHER takes out his jackknife and cuts the COW's throat. She is dead.*

BETH

(*angrily*) Operating on that cow was just stupid.

> *FATHER gets up quickly, grabs BETH by the shoulders, and slaps her in the face. BETH is stung. FATHER turns and begins to walk away. BETH picks up a handful of dirt and hurls it at her father. And another. And another.*

> *FATHER stops and pivots to face BETH. BETH runs for the door but doesn't get far before FATHER grabs her arm. He stares at Beth's dress. She looks down and realizes she is covered in dirt. A roaring sound begins.*

FATHER

Look at you, you're filthy. Get that dress off. Wash it!

> *BETH wrenches herself free of FATHER's grasp, ripping part of her dress in the process and falling to the ground. The roaring sound builds in intensity. FATHER stands over BETH. She struggles, but he holds her. FATHER undoes his belt, and – suddenly stops. The roaring stops. FILTHY BILLY has entered the barn. FATHER and BETH look at FILTHY BILLY.*

FILTHY BILLY

Went and forgot (shit) my canteen someplace. Don't know (fuck) where I (shit) put it.

> *FATHER rebuckles his belt, all the while watching FILTHY BILLY.*

FATHER

(*leaving the barn*) Crazy man.

> *Once FATHER has left, FILTHY BILLY goes to BETH and helps her up. He turns his back to her so she can rearrange her clothing.*

FILTHY BILLY

He doesn't know what he's doing.

BETH

He knew.

FILTHY BILLY

He won't remember. Or if he does, he won't know why he did it. You'll see.

BETH

I don't want to see him ever again.

> *BETH leans against the wall and hugs herself. FILTHY BILLY squats down beside her.*

BETH

Don't tell anyone.

FILTHY BILLY

No. That wouldn't do no good.

BETH
How did you know to come?

FILTHY BILLY
(*shrugging*) You got to be careful, you hear? Real careful.

BETH
You're not swearing.

FILTHY BILLY
Swearing? (*realizing*) Oh!

> *Suddenly the roaring sound is upon them again. FILTHY BILLY looks confused, backs away from BETH, and starts swatting some invisible thing away, as if he's being attacked by a swarm of wasps. Then he breaks into a torrent of swearing and scratching.*

BETH
Billy?

> *But FILTHY BILLY doesn't hear her. He runs out of the barn, batting away whatever is chasing him. BETH runs out of the barn after him.*

BETH
Billy!

> *But FILTHY BILLY is gone. BETH sees MOTHER in the yard. MOTHER notices BETH's torn dress.*

MOTHER
What have you done to your dress?

BETH
I —

MOTHER

Never mind your excuses. (*pause*) You can come to Kamloops with us. Perhaps we can find some material for a new dress there.

BETH perks up a little.

BETH

You mean it? What about school?

MOTHER

Hurry up; the democrat is loaded.

MOTHER climbs into the front of the democrat. BETH hops on the back.

BETH

Can I get some nylon stockings in Kamloops?

MOTHER

Nylon stockings! You're not old enough. *I* don't even have nylon stockings. Your father forbids that kind of wastefulness.

FATHER climbs into the front seat and takes CHERRY's reigns. He doesn't make eye contact with BETH, and BETH stays as far away from FATHER as possible.

MOTHER, FATHER, and BETH head off toward town in the democrat. They drive in silence along Blood Road, BETH still recovering from her encounter with FATHER. After a few moments, MOTHER points up ahead along the road.

MOTHER

Look. The turtles are out.

BETH stands up in the back of the cart to see what she's pointing at. Ahead, hundreds of painted TURTLES with yellow and olive-black shells cross the road in a slow, stubborn parade.

BETH
The turtles! Can I be the one to clear our path?

FATHER keeps driving forward toward the TURTLES.

BETH
Stop the cart, you'll run them over!

FATHER stares forward, determined. He slaps the reigns, forcing the horse forward.

MOTHER
John, stop.

BETH
STOP! YOU'LL KILL THEM!

But it's too late. The democrat runs right over the TURTLES. BETH closes her eyes tight but can't block out the crunch of the TURTLES being killed under the wheels of the cart, or CHERRY's whinnying.

As the democrat moves along, BETH looks back at the carnage.

BETH
(*to FATHER*) Why do you have to go around hurting things? I hate you.

MOTHER

> Enough. It's a long trip.

They ride off toward Kamloops.

....

SCENE 8

The next day. BETH sits on the tree stump. She reaches into her pocket and pulls out a tiny bottle of clear nail polish that her mother purchased for her in Kamloops. She finds the scrap of red velvet that is wrapped around her treasures. She pulls out her perfume and lipstick and adds the nail polish to the stash. She opens the nail polish and smells it. She paints one of her fingernails and gazes at it proudly. She interacts with her imaginary suitor once again.

BETH

> Why yes, Dennis, that *is* new nail polish. All the way from Kamloops. How kind of you to notice. Of course you may kiss my hand ... and my arm ... and my –

> *BETH hears a noise. Someone is coming. Panicking, she packs all of her treasures away. She climbs off the stump, but her sleeve gets caught. She struggles, only to get more entangled, scraping her arm in the process.*

> *BETH sees a motion in the grass; something is coming toward her. The grass splits as if a man or animal is running through it. She pulls harder on her sleeve, trying to escape. The swishing of grass gets louder and faster, and a roaring*

sound builds in intensity until: there he is, CRAZY JACK.
He's sweating and breathing heavily, and he has a crazed
look in his eyes. He looks toward BETH, then aggressively
tries to quiet the roaring sound.

JACK
Shhhhh. SHHHHHH!

Suddenly a hand is on BETH's shoulder, from behind. BETH
swings around to find NORA.

NORA
What's up?

BETH looks back, but CRAZY JACK is gone.

NORA
You okay? You got yourself stuck there.

NORA begins to untangle BETH.

NORA
You should do something about those scrapes.

BETH
They're okay.

NORA
Come on. We'll rinse 'em in the creek.

They go sit by a creek.

NORA
Shouldn't you be at school?

BETH doesn't respond.

NORA
The Georges' little girl's gone missing now too. She didn't
come home last night. My mum says I got to stay around the
reserve, don't go in the bush.

BETH
You're still out.

NORA washes Beth's scrapes. BETH flinches.

NORA
Lots of blood from nothing scratches. You won't die.

BETH
What do you think happened to the Georges' little girl?

NORA
Everybody's says it's Crazy Jack, but I don't think so.

BETH
Do you think Jack's got the evil Coyote spirit in him too?

NORA
(*laughing*) The evil Coyote spirit? Did Billy tell you that?
That's not what Coyote is. Coyote's a trickster. Sometimes
good, sometimes bad. Billy wants to believe Coyote killed his
dad. But Billy's dad was just a drunk.

BETH
So if it's not Jack, who's killing all these kids?

NORA
Something much worse. Something out for blood.

*NORA finishes cleaning BETH's wounds. Her fingers linger
on BETH's wrist.*

NORA

Your skin's so see-through. Like I could look inside and see your bones.

> *She looks up at BETH. There is a moment between the two of them. BETH breaks it.*

BETH

Wanna see something? A secret?

> *NORA nods eagerly. BETH leads NORA back to the tree stump. She reaches in and pulls out her red velvet packet of treasures and shows it to NORA.*

NORA

Where did you get all this?

BETH

Kamloops. My mum buys them for me. But I've got to hide them out here where my dad can't find them.

NORA

(examining the perfume bottle) What will he do?

BETH

I hid the perfume in my room once and he found it. He threw it in the manure pile.

NORA

(dropping the bottle) Ewwww!

BETH

I cleaned it up! *(holding up the lipstick)* Here, try this.

NORA

Has that been in the shit pile?

BETH
No!

NORA
Just checking.

BETH applies lipstick to NORA's lips.

BETH
You look beautiful!

NORA
Yeah? Like a city girl?

BETH
Definitely! Now do me!

NORA carefully applies lipstick to BETH's lips.

NORA
Perfect.

NORA leans in and kisses BETH on the lips. After the kiss, NORA looks directly at BETH, and BETH smiles.

BETH
(*emboldened by the kiss*) You know what we could do? We could catch the train this afternoon for Vancouver.

NORA
We don't have any money.

BETH
Don't need money. We could jump a train. Get a job in Vancouver as soon as we get there. We could go right now.

NORA

I dunno, that's pretty far away.

BETH

Come on!

NORA

My mum …

BETH

(*sulking*) Fine.

>*Silence. The magic of the previous moment is gone. NORA
>searches for a way to get it back.*

NORA

I could show you Crazy Jack's cabin. You ever been there?

BETH

Don't even know where it is.

NORA

I been there.

BETH

You're crazy.

NORA

Maybe. It's just a little house. Smaller than Dennis and
Billy's cabin. I looked in the window. Everything's really
tidy. He keeps a garden behind the cabin. I took a carrot and
ate it. Let's go there now.

BETH

I don't think so.

NORA

Come on!

>*NORA takes BETH's hand and leads her through the woods.*
>*The path is winding and steep. As they run, the forest is alive*
>*with wildlife. A FAWN drinks from the creek. The crashing*
>*of NORA and BETH's running startles the FAWN, and it*
>*darts for safety. BIRDS fly past the girls as they run.*
>
>*They arrive at a cabin. Their breath is short from the climb.*

BETH

What if he's home?

NORA

Are you scared?

>*BETH doesn't answer. NORA moves toward the cabin. BETH*
>*stays still.*

NORA

Come on.

BETH

I don't know.

NORA

Come on!

>*The girls sneak up to the cabin and peer in the window.*

NORA

He's out.

>*BETH is relieved, but before she can say anything, NORA*
>*opens the door and enters the cabin.*

BETH
Nora!

> *NORA just smiles at her and gestures for BETH to follow.*
> *BETH looks nervously around the meadow for signs of*
> *CRAZY JACK's return. Seeing no one, she tentatively*
> *follows NORA into the cabin. The cabin only contains a cot*
> *and a little table. On the table is a framed photograph of a*
> *young woman.*

NORA
See, I told you: tidy.

BETH
(*indicating the photo*) Who do you think that is?

NORA
I don't know.

BETH
Could be his wife.

NORA
Crazy Jack with a wife?

BETH
Could be. She could be dead. Or maybe she ran away. Maybe
he came up here cuz his heart was broken.

NORA
I can't see him with a woman of any kind.

BETH
Maybe it's his mum.

NORA

Maybe it's somebody else's picture. Somebody he doesn't know. He's so lonely, he stole some strange lady's photograph so he could make love to it. (*rubbing the photo all over her body and speaking as Crazy Jack*) Oh baby ... Oh yeah, baby, that's it ...

NORA is interrupted by a loud crashing sound, coming from the bush.

BETH

Someone's coming!

Panicked, NORA throws the photo on the bed, and she and BETH run out of the cabin, frantically looking in all directions. The crashing gets louder; it's almost at the cabin. The girls' hearts are pounding. There is nowhere for them to hide. Crazy Jack is sure to find them! And ...

The FAWN emerges from the woods.

NORA

Holy!

The FAWN stares at the girls, then runs off. The girls both laugh in relief.

BETH

I thought we were done for.

NORA

I wonder what she was warning us about?

BETH

Warning?

DENNIS sneaks up behind the girls. He puts one hand on each of their shoulders.

DENNIS

(*in a scary voice*) What are you kids doing here?

Both girls scream in fright. DENNIS laughs.

NORA

(*swatting at him*) Dennis!

DENNIS

You two shouldn't come up here. It's not safe. Crazy Jack's not well.

BETH

We didn't do anything. (*unconvincingly*) I mean, we didn't go inside his house or anything.

NORA looks at BETH incredulously.

DENNIS

You gotta be careful in the bush. You'll end up like the Georges' kid or that Kemp girl. There's something picking off kids.

NORA

(*to DENNIS*) What are you doing here, anyway?

DENNIS

What are *you* doing here? Bit far from the reserve, ain't ya? Does your mum know?

NORA

(*relenting*) Nah.

DENNIS
(*putting his arm around BETH and smiling at NORA*) Me,
I gotta keep my girlfriend safe from trouble.

NORA
Girlfriend?

BETH
I ... I –

DENNIS
You bet.

> *DENNIS kisses BETH on the cheek. NORA looks to BETH*
> *for confirmation. BETH, not knowing how to react, looks*
> *sheepishly back at NORA. NORA sulks.*

. . . .

SCENE 9

> *BETH returns home. MOTHER is in the kitchen.*

BETH
I'm home!

MOTHER
How was school today?

BETH
Oh good. We –

MOTHER
Mrs. Boulee says you haven't been to school in a week.

BETH searches for a response.

MOTHER

I had to lie. I told her we needed your help on the farm. How many times do I have to lie for you?

BETH

You don't have to lie.

MOTHER

Where have you been? Have you been with Dennis?

BETH

I haven't been with anybody.

MOTHER

You're lying to me. Tell me the truth.

BETH

I am telling the truth. Sometimes I'm with that Indian girl, Nora. Only Nora.

MOTHER

Does she make you miss school? Answer me!

BETH

The kids pick on me. They call me "sheep tick" and "Indian lover."

MOTHER

Tell me the truth!

BETH

What good is it telling the truth if you're not going to believe me?

MOTHER

Tell me where you've been all day, where you go.

BETH

Out walking.

MOTHER

You go to the reserve?

BETH

Sometimes. Sometimes I just walk.

MOTHER

You don't see Dennis?

BETH

No! I just walk. Sometimes I see Nora and we do things.

MOTHER

Things? What things?

BETH

Nothing! Just leave me alone!

MOTHER turns and stares at BETH.

MOTHER

Did Dennis get inside you?

BETH

No!

MOTHER

Did Dennis get inside you? Answer me!

BETH

No!

MOTHER continues to stare at BETH, assessing her.

MOTHER
We've got to clean you up.

MOTHER mixes vinegar and water together in a wine bottle, muttering to her dead mother all the while. MOTHER hands the bottle to BETH.

MOTHER
You know what it is to douche?

BETH nods.

MOTHER
Go to the outhouse and douche with that.

BETH
Why?

MOTHER
Just do it. It will help stop anything that might have started.

BETH
What do you mean?

MOTHER
Just go do it. Take a towel. (*pause*) If a boy got inside you, ever gets inside of you, you take care of it. Understand? You're too young for mothering. Too young for any of it.

BETH
(*embarrassed and confused*) I didn't do anything. I won't do anything.

MOTHER

> I don't want to hear about it. I don't ever want to hear
> about it.

MOTHER exits, leaving BETH standing in the kitchen,
holding the wine bottle, confused and ashamed.

....

SCENE 10

BETH's bedroom. Night. It's dark; the room is only lit by
the moonlight coming in the window. We see the shape of
BETH in the bed, the shape of the forget-me-nots painted
on her walls.

The slam of the screen door. FATHER enters the house from
outside, drunk, stumbling and muttering to himself. He
walks to BETH's room and stops in the doorframe. We see
only his silhouette. He stands in the doorframe for a few
moments, watching. BETH remains still. The rocks outside
begin to rattle.

FATHER approaches the bed. His shadow is on the wall.
As he approaches, his shadow transforms into that of a
coyote. The coyote climbs onto BETH's bed. The forget-me-
nots on the wall begin to tangle and grow into menacing
underbrush. The coyote howls.

In silhouette, BETH's arm shoots up to protect her. The
coyote sinks his teeth into her arm. She cries out sharply in
pain. The coyote begins to devour Beth's arm. She struggles

quietly. Once the coyote has ingested her arm, it devours the rest of her body, fully. Silence. The coyote snarls and howls, then retreats. As the coyote steps off the bed, the shadow returns to form of FATHER, and the menacing underbrush recedes. FATHER stands in silhouette in the doorframe for a moment, watching BETH, then stumbles off to his armchair in the living room.

Silence. Stillness.

BETH stands and slowly walks from her room into the kitchen. She picks up the wine bottle filled with vinegar solution. She walks out of the house, headed for the outhouse, carrying the bottle. Outside she sees LUCIFER sitting on the grass, staring at her. He is surprisingly calm. He is not walking in circles.

BETH
What do you want?

LUCIFER tilts his head and walks forward toward BETH.

BETH
Get out of here.

BETH kicks at the cat. He scurries back. She charges at the cat angrily.

BETH
Get out of here! GET OUT OF HERE!

LUCIFER runs away. Silence.

BETH screams, long and loudly, with the power of many voices. Even when she stops screaming, the sound lingers on, bestial and lonely.

BETH takes a few steps toward the outhouse, then stops, turns and runs into the woods.

. . . .

SCENE 11

The next morning. BETH sleeps in the grass beside the tree stump. NORA arrives and discovers BETH, asleep. NORA leans her face in very close to BETH's and breathes her in. BETH opens her eyes and jumps up, startled.

NORA
What are you doing here?

BETH
(*loudly*) What are you doing here?

NORA
You don't have to yell.

    Beat.

NORA
So you going to tell me what happened last night?

BETH
Nothing happened.

NORA

Really? Just felt like sleeping in the woods?

BETH doesn't respond.

NORA

Your dad?

BETH

Never mind.

BETH is silent for a moment.

NORA

What's the matter with you today? (*pause*) I seen Dennis and you.

BETH

When?

NORA

I seen.

BETH

You haven't seen anything.

NORA

I seen.

BETH

Maybe you're a spy like them Germans, or them Japs. Maybe you're a Jap spy.

NORA

You like him better than me.

BETH

Don't be so silly.

NORA

Let's go. You said those factories in Vancouver will hire any woman who shows up on the doorstep. I wanna go. With you.

BETH

You didn't want to go before.

NORA

I do now!

BETH

Nobody's going to hire fifteen-year-old girls.

NORA

We'll say we're eighteen. We'll wear makeup. Nobody will know. You can wear this!

NORA pulls a tube of lipstick from her pocket.

BETH

Where did you get this?

NORA

My mother bought it for me.

BETH

She did not. You stole it.

NORA

What does it matter where I got it? Try it on.

BETH

No.

NORA

We could go anywhere. We could jump the train and just go!

BETH

I don't know. We don't have any money.

NORA

Granny does.

BETH

I'm not stealing from your granny.

NORA

We could go tonight.

BETH

I'm not ready to go.

NORA

Why not? You were ready before. What're you staying for?
A crazy father? Mother who talks to herself? Or are you
staying for Dennis?

BETH

I'm not staying for Dennis.

NORA

Who then?

BETH

I should get back.

NORA

Maybe Dennis will buy you a present, eh? Maybe that's why
you're his girlfriend, cuz he pays for it?

NORA walks away, leaving BETH alone at the tree stump. BETH is angry, defeated, and alone. She reaches into the tree stump and pulls out her velvet packet. She throws the lipstick, perfume, and nail polish into the trees. She turns and begins to walk away. In the trees in front of her, she sees CRAZY JACK. She freezes. CRAZY JACK holds out his hand, offering her something. BETH slowly moves toward him. She sees he's holding the lipstick she threw into the woods.

BETH

(*tentatively*) For me? (*pause*) For me? (*moving closer to him, until she can take the lipstick from his hand*) Thank you. (*pause*) Did you kill Sarah Kemp and those other kids?

Then, suddenly, CRAZY JACK disappears back into the trees. BETH watches him go, then looks down at the lipstick in her hand.

. . . .

SCENE 12

BETH arrives at the house and enters the kitchen. She holds a bunch of wildflowers. MOTHER is working in the kitchen. BETH holds out the wildflowers as an offering.

BETH

These are for you.

MOTHER

Should I ask where you've been?

BETH shakes her head. MOTHER wipes her hands on her apron and takes the flowers. She holds them to her face and breathes in. For a moment, her face relaxes. MOTHER pinches a flower from the bunch and presses it in her scrapbook.

MOTHER
There. Something to remember the day by. Though Lord knows why I want to remember it.

MOTHER puts the rest of the wildflowers in a canning jar filled with water and returns to her work. BETH looks through the scrapbook. She discovers a tortoiseshell butterfly pressed flat on the same page, the bottom of one wing torn away.

BETH
A butterfly. What happened to its wing?

MOTHER
I kept it because of its torn wing. Wonderful. That it could still fly. A reminder to keep going.

BETH touches the butterfly.

MOTHER
I asked you not to touch that. How many times do I have to tell you?

BETH pulls her hand back.

MOTHER
Get the coffee ready; the men will be in soon.

MOTHER leaves the kitchen. BETH watches her go, and, when the coast is clear, BETH sneaks another look at the scrapbook. She leafs through the book. FILTHY BILLY enters quietly from the yard and watches BETH for a moment.

FILTHY BILLY

You should (shit) leave that alone.

BETH

(*surprised at being caught*) What?

FILTHY BILLY

(*nodding toward the scrapbook*) That's (fuck) your mother's private place. Everybody needs a place to sort things out (fuck).

BETH

It's not like a diary.

FILTHY BILLY

Doesn't (shit) matter what's in it. (Fuck) Excuse me.

BETH takes a scrawled note out of the scrapbook.

BETH

(*reading aloud*) "The Cure for Death by Lightning: Dunk the dead by lightning in a cold-water bath for two hours and, if still dead, add vinegar and soak for an hour more."

FILTHY BILLY

(*laughing*) Do you think that (fuck) would work?

BETH laughs. FATHER and DENNIS enter from the yard. BETH quickly closes the scrapbook. MOTHER enters, and the kitchen is now alive with activity. BETH serves the men coffee and cake.

FATHER

Don't know what's gotten into that Swede. He was standing across the street when I came out of the blacksmith's, like he was waiting for me. But all he did was stare.

DENNIS

Did you talk to him?

FATHER

Nothing to talk about.

DENNIS

No, you're right. You go out late at night, tear down his fence, and put up your own. And then the next day the Swede tears down yours and puts his back up. Nothing to talk about.

FATHER grunts.

BETH

Mr. Johannsen warned me that he'd do something if you didn't stop taking down the fence.

FATHER

When was this?

BETH

A while ago.

FATHER

Why didn't you tell me?

BETH
You'd yell. You always yell.

FATHER
(*yelling*) I don't yell! (*quietly*) I wouldn't yell.

Everyone eats in silence for a moment.

DENNIS
(*to MOTHER*) You like your nylon stockings okay?

MOTHER
Nylon stockings?

FATHER shakes his head.

DENNIS
I guess I spoiled the surprise. John got me to pick some up for you.

MOTHER looks at FATHER, and FATHER looks down at his coffee. FILTHY BILLY's swearing swirls up into a flurry and dies down again.

MOTHER
You bought them for Beth?

FATHER doesn't respond. MOTHER becomes enraged.

MOTHER
You bought them for Beth!

MOTHER storms away from the table, muttering to someone only she can see. FILTHY BILLY grows more agitated, swearing, scratching, and shifting in his chair. Finally …

FATHER

(*to the hired hands*) Well let's get that binder fixed. We've got work to do.

DENNIS

But we just –

FATHER

Now!

> *The men stand and get ready to head out to work.*
> *MOTHER sits in her rocking chair, clutching her scrapbook*
> *and staring off into the distance. FATHER and FILTHY*
> *BILLY exit to the field. DENNIS squeezes BETH's shoulder*
> *and follows them.*

BETH

Mum, do you want some tea or something?

> *MOTHER continues rocking and muttering. BETH reaches*
> *out to touch MOTHER's cheek, but MOTHER pulls away.*
> *BETH goes to her room to retrieve the nylon stockings. She*
> *brings them to the kitchen. She places the stockings on the*
> *table in front of her mother.*

BETH

You see the nylon stockings, Mum? For you.

> *Beat.*

MOTHER

My father gave me stockings too – silk stockings – while my mother went without.

> *BETH stops for a moment, but doesn't want to acknowledge*
> *what her mother has said.*

SCENE 13

Late at night. Outside the farmhouse. BETH looks for LUCIFER.

BETH

Lucifer ... Lucifer! (*stopping in her tracks, seeing that the field is ablaze*) Fire! Fire!

MOTHER and FATHER emerge from the house, MOTHER still clutching her scrapbook.

MOTHER

Beth! Oh Beth!

BETH

I'll get Billy and Dennis!

BETH turns to run, but FILTHY BILLY is already there. FILTHY BILLY hands BETH a handful of milk buckets.

FILTHY BILLY

You fill these. I'll get the shovels.

BETH

Where's Dennis?

FILTHY BILLY

Drunk.

MOTHER is holding FATHER's shirt sleeve. No matter how he twists and turns, she won't let him go.

MOTHER

You will stay here! You will help put this fire out!

FATHER

Let go of me! That Swede!

MOTHER

That Swede nothing. There'll be nothing to come back to if we can't hold the fire. Don't be a fool, for heaven's sake!

FILTHY BILLY marches up to FATHER with a shovel.

FILTHY BILLY

Take this! We have to get this fire under control.

FATHER resists. FILTHY BILLY forces the shovel into his hand.

FILTHY BILLY

Come with me. Now!

He grabs FATHER by the arm, and the two of them run into the field. Both MOTHER and BETH are surprised and impressed. We see the black silhouettes of the two men shoveling blackness onto bright orange flames sending sparks showering into the sky. BETH pumps water furiously as MOTHER carries and pours buckets.

Eventually the fire recedes to a more manageable burn. FATHER drops his shovel and marches into the house. FILTHY BILLY, BETH, and MOTHER continue working to put out the fire. FATHER emerges from the house carrying a tin of kerosene and a gun. He exits, walking toward the Swede's farm. MOTHER returns to the pump for more water.

BETH

    He's gone to Mr. Johannsen's. He took the kerosene. And
    the gun.

MOTHER

    Oh Lord.

BETH

    We should do something.

MOTHER

    What can we do? Help Billy with the fire. I'll ride to Boulee's.
    We can't stop him alone.

       *MOTHER exits. BETH continues pumping. FILTHY BILLY
       returns with empty buckets and grabs the ones BETH has
       filled. He runs off again. BETH keeps pumping. The roaring
       sound starts and CRAZY JACK crashes into the clearing,
       carrying a torch.*

BETH

    Jack!

       *CRAZY JACK turns and sees BETH. He holds his torch to the
       flax that is growing in the field, spreading more fire.*

BETH

    No! Stop! Billy, help!

       CRAZY JACK stops, looks at his torch, confused, and drops it.

BETH

    Dad! Mum! Help!

       CRAZY JACK grabs BETH and covers her mouth.

CRAZY JACK
    Shhh. Shhhh!

      CRAZY JACK wrestles BETH to the ground as the torch he dropped lights more of the crop ablaze. Suddenly a gunshot rings out from the direction of the Swede's farm. BETH and CRAZY JACK stop struggling and look back to the sound of the shot.

      CRAZY JACK stands, then yells something incoherent. He swings around as if fighting some invisible force, then runs off into the night.

      Frozen with fear, BETH watches him go. The field continues to burn.

      End of Act 1.

ACT 2

....

SCENE 1

Later that night. The fire has gone out. BETH is exhausted.
She sits on the porch staring out at the night. FILTHY
BILLY returns and watches her.

FILTHY BILLY
You okay?

BETH
Crazy Jack set the fire. Why would he do that?

FILTHY BILLY
Something's (shit) wrong with him.

BETH
He looked so – like an animal.

FILTHY BILLY
He's lived too long in the bush. The bush makes you (fuck)
change shape. Takes away your man-body, makes you into an
animal. Coyote's took him over (shit).

BETH
I think he's following me.

FILTHY BILLY

He's (fuck) dangerous. You gotta be careful.

FILTHY BILLY sits beside BETH. His presence comforts her.

BETH

That was something, you taking over with the fire. Telling my father what to do. He doesn't let anyone tell him what to do.

FILTHY BILLY

He was (shit) surprised. (Fuck) Sorry. He's easier (shit) on me than Dennis 'cause (fuck) he thinks I'm slow.

BETH

You been tricking him? The swearing, I mean?

FILTHY BILLY

That's (shit) no trick. I feel bad (shit), you know. (Fuck) It's dirty.

BETH

I don't mind. It's kind of funny.

They sit in silence for a moment. NORA arrives and sees them sitting together.

NORA

They've taken your dad to jail!

BETH

Who? What do you mean?

NORA

Some men. I think they were Mounties. They came in a car and took him away.

BETH

My mother?

NORA

She's the one that got them to take him away.

BETH

What are you talking about?

NORA

When I got there, they were putting the Swede's body in the back of a buggy and driving him off. Must've been dead. Your dad looked crazy. Some guys handcuffed him and put him in the car. He's gone!

BETH turns away.

NORA

Hey, what's the matter? He'll get it for murder. They'll lock him up!

FILTHY BILLY

He's still her (shit) father.

NORA

He's a monster. (*to BETH*) Don't you see? We can go! We can get out of here right now! Nobody's going to know until we're so far away they can't find us.

BETH

Maybe you should go. I've got to do chores.

NORA

Aw, come on. This is our chance!

FILTHY BILLY
(Shit) I think (fuck) you should go.

NORA
Shut up.

BETH
Please, Nora, I don't want you here when Mum comes back.

NORA
Fine.

> *NORA storms off. BETH and FILTHY BILLY watch her go.*
> *MOTHER returns home.*

BETH
Mum! What happened?

> *MOTHER crumples to the ground. BETH runs to her and*
> *holds her.*

MOTHER
They've taken your father away.

BETH
Is Mr. Johannsen dead?

MOTHER
Dead? No, he was drunk.

BETH
What's going to happen? With Dad?

MOTHER
I don't know.

*MOTHER closes her eyes and begins to mutter to her dead
mother. BETH and FILTHY BILLY help MOTHER up and
walk her into the house.*

. . . .

SCENE 2

Kitchen. MOTHER, DENNIS, and BETH at the table.

MOTHER
There's work for you and Billy right through the winter if
you want it.

DENNIS grins and nods.

DENNIS
How's John?

MOTHER
He's fine. He's got a job at the mill. He's living up there, in
the camp. He'll be there 'til spring.

DENNIS
You don't have to lie to me. I know where he is.

MOTHER
I'm not lying. He's at the mill.

DENNIS
There's no shame in it. That place will keep him from making more trouble.

BETH looks on anxiously.

BETH

Where is he? Where?

*MOTHER stands from the table and busies herself at the
sink. DENNIS leans in to BETH.*

DENNIS

With all the mentals.

DENNIS laughs. BETH runs to her mother.

BETH

Is that where he is?

MOTHER

I don't want to talk about it. (*pause*) Yes, and I don't want
anyone to know. Do you understand?

BETH

It looks like everyone knows already. Except me.

MOTHER

(*to DENNIS*) I'd like you and Billy to finish off Mr.
Johannsen's fence. But I'd like you to keep it between
yourselves.

DENNIS

Why?

MOTHER

It doesn't matter why.

DENNIS

So John don't find out, eh? Let him think he won the war.

MOTHER

I'd rather we kept it to ourselves.

DENNIS

It's a bad time of year for digging fence posts.

MOTHER

Will you do it, or not?

DENNIS nods.

MOTHER

Good. We'll put this matter with Johannsen to rest once and for all. (*to BETH and DENNIS*) But you stay away from each other. Understand me? I'll have enough work to keep you both very busy.

BETH blushes.

BETH

What's going to happen to Dad?

Beat.

MOTHER

I don't know what's going to happen. He won't be home for a long time. (*pause*) We're going into town tomorrow.

DENNIS

You think that's a good idea?

MOTHER

There's cream to go in, and there's things we need. Finish up. There is work to be done.

MOTHER strides out of the room.

BETH

He's at the mental hospital?

DENNIS

You know what Billy says? He says your daddy met Coyote in the mountains, last spring when that bear attacked your camp. Coyote got hold of him then. Made John act like a wild man. He gets some crazy ideas, that Billy. But the way your dad was acting, maybe Billy's right. (*moving closer to BETH with a smile*) Seein' as I'm staying on here, looks like you can still be my girlfriend. Maybe we can pick up where we left off, eh? (*sliding his hand up BETH's arm and touching her face*)

BETH

(*pulling away from DENNIS*) I can't. My mum ...

DENNIS

Don't keep me waiting too long.

> *DENNIS exits. BETH sits alone.*

....

SCENE 3

> *BETH walks through the woods looking for NORA. She finds NORA sitting at the tree stump, holding a knife. They stand in silence for a moment.*

BETH

Sorry I had to tell you to go.

NORA

Sorry I got so mad.

BETH

That's okay.

Beat.

BETH

Why are you out so late?

NORA

My mum went into hysterics. Tore my stuff apart.

BETH

What's she mad about?

NORA

(*shrugging*) Doesn't want me walking in the bush.

BETH

Why?

NORA

She says my father was some white man working for the
Fergusons, who caught her in the bush.

BETH

Well of course she doesn't like you out walking then.

NORA

She doesn't like me doing nothing. She'll hit me if I look at
her cross-eyed. She learned how to hit from them teachers at
the school.

Beat.

BETH

Want to try on my lipstick?

NORA

Nah.

They both look up at the moon in silence.

NORA

Granny says the moon is a woman and the woman gives birth to herself over and over.

BETH

You can't give birth to yourself.

Beat.

NORA

Have you been with Dennis?

BETH

No! Is that what he told you?

NORA

He wouldn't tell me nothing. So I figured something happened. He tells lies about girls if nothing happened and says nothing if something did.

BETH

What girls?

NORA

Jealous?

BETH

No.

Beat.

NORA

If he hurts you, I'll beat him up. I'll knife him.

BETH

Yeah, sure.

NORA closes her knife and puts it in her pocket.

NORA

I love you, Beth Weeks.

BETH

I know it.

NORA looks at BETH, then turns and disappears into the woods. BETH watches her go.

. . . .

SCENE 4

Night. Late autumn, nearing winter. MOTHER and BETH are doing dishes in the kitchen. DENNIS stumbles in, smelling of booze and grinning like a lunatic. He sits and puts his feet up on the table. MOTHER looks at him disapprovingly but doesn't say anything.

DENNIS

Well! How's everybody tonight?

DENNIS laughs loudly. MOTHER pours DENNIS a mug of coffee and slams it on the table. DENNIS downs the cup of coffee and holds the cup out for more. MOTHER fills his cup. DENNIS looks at BETH with a frank desire that makes BETH uncomfortable. MOTHER sees this.

MOTHER
Get your feet off the table.

DENNIS
I ain't hurting nothing.

MOTHER
I don't like it.

DENNIS does not take his feet down.

DENNIS
I went to town today.

MOTHER
I see that.

DENNIS
Bumped into the doc. He wanted me to tell you that John's allowed to have visitors. Wondered why you haven't been yet. He thought you might not know.

DENNIS laughs long and hard. MOTHER pushes his feet off the table, and DENNIS falls. He lets out a whoop as he hits the floor.

MOTHER
I've had enough of this. Get out. Go home and sober up.

DENNIS
Okay, okay. I'm going.

DENNIS heaves himself clumsily off the floor. He rubs his face, trying to sober up.

DENNIS

I'm sorry. It's the booze talking. Billy's getting a good fire going. Why don't you both come over for the fire?

MOTHER

Sober up. I won't have a drunk working for me.

DENNIS

Okay! All right!

DENNIS exits the house.

BETH

We can visit?

MOTHER

No.

BETH

But Dennis said –

MOTHER

Never mind what Dennis said.

BETH

Why haven't you gone to see him?

MOTHER

I can't.

BETH

I'm sure he wants to see you.

MOTHER

I can't.

BETH

But maybe if we visit it'll help him get better.

MOTHER

(*exploding*) He's not going to get better!

> *BETH is horrified. She begins to sob. MOTHER calms herself and takes in BETH's state. MOTHER opens her scrapbook. She looks for a specific page, finds it, grabs a couple of ingredients from the shelf, and quickly stirs them together in a bowl. BETH continues to cry. MOTHER holds the bowl under BETH's nose.*

MOTHER

Breathe this in. It will calm you.

> *BETH turns away and continues to sob.*

MOTHER

Breathe.

> *BETH relents. She puts her head over the bowl and breathes in a few times. Her sobs subside to whimpers, until she's finally got herself back under control.*

BETH

There are times I hate him. And times I wish he would walk through the door.

MOTHER

All this talking and crying is going to get us nowhere. You be strong. Your father will be fine. Let's go to the bonfire.

MOTHER grabs her coat. She heads for the door and turns back to BETH.

MOTHER
Bring the gun.

MOTHER exits. BETH grabs the gun off the rack and follows.

. . . .

SCENE 5

MOTHER and BETH approach the bonfire outside of DENNIS and FILTHY BILLY's cabin. DENNIS leaps crazily, clumsily in a circle around the fire, tripping and righting himself, singing out and stopping to drink from the bottle in his hand. It's obvious he's drunker than before. FILTHY BILLY, as sober as ever, feeds the fire and teases up the flames. DENNIS sees MOTHER and BETH approach.

DENNIS
Ladies! I knew you'd come!

DENNIS falls sloppily to the ground.

BETH
(*to FILTHY BILLY about DENNIS*) Is he all right?

FILTHY BILLY
Stupid. Shouldn't have gotten drunk (shit). He knows better. Booze makes you weak.

DENNIS starts crawling around on his belly, scrambling after FILTHY BILLY.

DENNIS

I'm a lizard! Watch out, Billy, I'M GOING TO EAT YOUR HEART!

DENNIS grabs for FILTHY BILLY, FILTHY BILLY steps out of the way, and DENNIS falls, face-first, into the dirt. He is knocked out cold. FILTHY BILLY turns DENNIS over and props his head on a mound of dirt so he can sleep. NORA arrives at the fire and sees BETH.

NORA

Beth!

NORA runs to hug BETH, but stops as she gets closer and sees MOTHER.

NORA

(*awkwardly*) Oh hi.

BETH

Nora, this is my mum.

NORA

(*strangely formal*) How do you do, Mrs. Weeks? It is very pleasurable to meet you.

MOTHER

So you're the Nora that Beth spends all her time with.

NORA

(*not sure whether that's good or bad*) I guess so.

MOTHER

(*with a smile*) It is very pleasurable to meet you as well, Nora.

MOTHER invites NORA to sit at the fire with her.

MOTHER

Beth says you live with your mother.

NORA

I do. Beth says you talk to your mother.

BETH

Nora!

NORA

(*realizing her mistake*) Sorry!

MOTHER

My mother always said she would contact me from the other side, and she did. She's still with me. We talk. She advises me.

NORA

You're a lucky woman to have your mother advising you still.

MOTHER

(*deciding to share*) When I was a girl, we would have seances for fun in the evenings. We'd sit around a table and join hands, my sisters and me, and try to contact the dead. There were books on how to do it: what to wear, what to eat before, how to hold your hands.

BETH

(*wanting her mother to stop*) Mum.

NORA

Did you see anything? Were there spirits?

MOTHER

There were knocks under the table once, but it could have been my sisters playing a trick. I thought I saw a ghost in my room, at the foot of my bed, when I was a girl, no older than Beth's age. I was sure of it then.

NORA

And now?

MOTHER

Memory ... You can never be sure, can you? This is nice. You should join us for Christmas this year, Nora. It would be lovely to have you.

NORA beams at BETH. A coyote howls and yips nearby,
followed by the sounds of SHEEP.

FILTHY BILLY

Sounds like there's another coyote getting at the sheep. He'll eat a few of them if we don't stop him.

BETH

(*grabbing her gun*) Come on, Billy, we'll scare him off. (*to MOTHER and NORA*) We'll be right back. You two have fun.

FILTHY BILLY and BETH leave MOTHER and NORA
at the fire and head out into the darkness. As they walk,
FILTHY BILLY talks.

FILTHY BILLY

(Fuck) You be careful with Dennis when he's drunk.

BETH

Yeah, yeah.

FILTHY BILLY

I mean it.

BETH

He looks ridiculous. Scrambling around pretending he's
a liz–

> *FILTHY BILLY holds his hand out to stop BETH. He points
> to the ground.*

FILTHY BILLY

Look. Dead sheep.

> *BETH looks down and sees the dead SHEEP. The SHEEP's
> belly is scarlet with blood, where it has been torn open
> and eaten by a coyote. BETH puts her hand to her mouth,
> disturbed at the sight.*

FILTHY BILLY

Ate her stomach right off.

> *And then, a sound. A rushing.*

FILTHY BILLY

He's coming.

BETH

Who's coming?

> *The SHEEP split and run in two directions, opening a path
> between them that runs straight at BETH and BILLY. The
> sound becomes deafening.*

BETH

Billy! What's happening? Who's coming?

Panicked, BETH shoots the gun into the air, unsure of what to aim at. FILTHY BILLY holds his ears against the sound and falls to his knees.

FILTHY BILLY

No. Please, no.

The sound is upon them, engulfing them. FILTHY BILLY falls over and goes into convulsions. BETH drops the gun and kneels beside him.

BETH

Billy? Are you all right, Billy?

BETH holds his head and smoothes back his hair. FILTHY BILLY's body jerks frantically. Finally the sound dies down and FILTHY BILLY's convulsions stop. He begins to swear.

BETH

You okay?

FILTHY BILLY

(Shit) I'm all right.

BETH

What happened?

FILTHY BILLY

Coyote (fuck) came back. Let's go back to the fire (shit).

BETH

What knocked you over? I didn't see anything out there. I didn't see any coyote. Was it the coyote that killed the sheep?

FILTHY BILLY

(Fuck) You don't have to name it Coyote if you don't want. (Shit) You can call it demon or ghost, but it's out here. (*pause*) Coyote (fuck) goes for the weak ones (shit). He goes for Crazy Jack, your father, (shit) and now he's out walking. We should go. It's not safe here.

> *BETH helps FILTHY BILLY up, and they walk. BETH looks nervously around as she supports FILTHY BILLY.*

. . . .

SCENE 6

Christmas. Snow falls. BETH hangs a wreath on the front door. She hears a sound: rocks rattling. She looks over to the rocks. MOTHER emerges from inside, holding a gift in her hand.

BETH

(*to MOTHER*) What's this?

MOTHER

Open it.

> *BETH unwraps the present excitedly. It's a bar of of sweet-smelling soap. BETH breathes deeply, enjoying the scent. She hugs her mother.*

BETH

Soap! Thank you, Mum! It smells wonderful!

MOTHER

You're very welcome. Merry Christmas.

MOTHER kisses BETH on the head. MOTHER and BETH work together to decorate the porch with evergreen boughs and ribbon.

BETH

I miss Dad singing Christmas carols. His low, rumbly voice.

MOTHER

He did love to sing.

BETH

And he would make up words for the parts he didn't know. (*singing*) "Later on, we'll perspire / we're too close to the fire."

BETH and MOTHER laugh.

BETH

Will he ever come back?

MOTHER

Someday.

BETH

But will the old Dad ever come back? The one who sang Christmas carols? You said he'd never get better.

MOTHER

I was just tired. Don't listen to me. I'm sure he'll be right as rain when he returns.

BETH wants to press her mother for more answers but is interrupted by DENNIS's arrival.

DENNIS

Merry Christmas! (*holding up a dead porcupine*) I brought chicken!

MOTHER

(*laughing*) Not in my house!

> *DENNIS disposes of the porcupine. MOTHER goes inside.*

DENNIS

I got you something too.

BETH

Thank you.

> *DENNIS hands her a gift wrapped in a flour sack. She opens it cautiously and discovers nylon stockings. BETH looks up to DENNIS who gives her a wink.*

DENNIS

Nylons. Can't wait to see you wear 'em.

> *Embarrassed, BETH looks away. She quickly squirrels the stockings away before her mother can see them. NORA arrives in the yard. BETH crosses away from DENNIS toward NORA.*

NORA

(*to BETH*) Merry Christmas!

BETH

Nora! Merry Christmas!

NORA

(*to DENNIS*) Merry Christmas!

DENNIS

Merry Christmas, cousin!

MOTHER emerges from the house to greet NORA.

NORA

Merry Christmas!

MOTHER

Same to you, Nora.

BETH

(*blurting out*) What did the homesteader children die of?

Everyone is surprised by this outburst.

BETH

The ones buried here in our yard. What did they die of?

MOTHER

Why do you want to know that now?

BETH shrugs.

MOTHER

I guess they died of the usual things. Whooping cough, measles, fever.

BETH

(*to NORA*) You said they died like Sarah Kemp.

NORA

They did. They were found all chewed up. People said it was a bear that got the kids. But it wasn't. The thing that got those kids is still out there walking the mountains.

MOTHER

This is not Christmas conversation. Let's head inside.

DENNIS

You're right. (*looking at BETH*) Maybe we should go inside, enjoy our gifts, try them on.

> *BETH blushes. NORA points at the side of the barn, where CRAZY JACK stands.*

NORA

Crazy Jack.

> *They all look.*

MOTHER

He isn't spending Christmas with Johannsen?

DENNIS

Never does. Won't even talk to the Swede. Runs off whenever he gets near.

MOTHER

Beth, see if you can invite him in.

BETH

I don't want to go anywhere near him. He's crazy.

MOTHER

Beth!

BETH

He lit the fire!

MOTHER

We need to start being good neighbours.

> MOTHER, DENNIS, and NORA head inside. BETH stays on
> the porch, keeping her distance from CRAZY JACK.

BETH

(*to CRAZY JACK*) My mum wants to know if you want to
come in for Christmas.

> CRAZY JACK slinks away into the shadows.

BETH

(*to herself*) Good.

> BETH stands on the porch in the cold air for a moment.
> Eventually NORA comes outside and holds BETH's hand.

NORA

You should come inside. You're cold.

> FILTHY BILLY walks across the field. He's all cleaned
> up, wearing a suit. His hair is slicked back and he's
> cleanly shaven.

FILTHY BILLY

Merry Christmas! (Fuck) Excuse me!

BETH

Merry Christmas!

> FILTHY BILLY hands a burlap bundle to BETH. She
> unties the string holding the bundle together. The burlap
> falls away, and BETH discovers she is holding an entire
> buttercup plant – dirt, roots, and delicate, yellow petals.

BETH

Where did you find this?

FILTHY BILLY shrugs and grins.

FILTHY BILLY
(Shit) In the snow. I found it (fuck) a week ago, and I said,
"That's what I'm giving Beth for Christmas (shit) because
that's how (shit) she makes me feel. She's the bright spot
in the snow." (Fuck)

BETH
It's beautiful!

*BETH gives FILTHY BILLY a peck on the cheek. NORA
huffs off into the woods, sulking. BETH chooses to ignore
NORA's sulking and sits on the porch steps with FILTHY
BILLY instead.*

*CRAZY JACK sidles up to the edge of the barn. FILTHY
BILLY points him out, and CRAZY JACK immediately
disappears.*

BETH
He keeps turning up. I don't know what he wants.

FILTHY BILLY
He's (shit) sweet on you.

BETH
Oh no, not him!

FILTHY BILLY
Sure. Dennis wants you for his girlfriend too. And Nora
(fuck). Others, I bet.

*BETH and FILTHY BILLY don't look at each other – but
their hands find each other. They hold hands and stare into*

the distance with the sound of the Christmas party behind
them. They sit like this for a few moments until, finally,
FILTHY BILLY says:

FILTHY BILLY

I want to show you something.

Holding hands, FILTHY BILLY and BETH walk into the
bush, close to the house. FILTHY BILLY points at a boulder
sticking up from the snow.

FILTHY BILLY

This (fuck) is where my father died. That's his stone.

BETH

I didn't know.

FILTHY BILLY

(Shit) He was Coyote's house, see? Coyote (fuck) never
made my father do bad things like he makes some other men
do. He was Coyote's resting place. Once, when Coyote was
resting inside him, (fuck, shit) my father took his own life –
so Coyote would have to return to the spirit world with him
(shit). But Coyote came back. And now I'm his house.

BETH

His house?

FILTHY BILLY

(Fuck) His safe place. But sometimes (shit), like now, he
takes off. (Shit) If he gets inside the wrong person, that's
a problem. I chase him down, find out (fuck) who he's in,
and try to stop whatever he's up to. But (shit) I'm tiring out.
I can't keep up. My father took Coyote with him when (shit)
he killed himself. (Fuck) That's the only way.

BETH

You're not thinking of that.

FILTHY BILLY

I don't know. I don't (shit) know no other way.

BETH

Billy, no!

FILTHY BILLY

I don't want (shit) any of this. I'm not brave like (shit) my father, if that's what it was. Maybe he was just an old drunk. (Fuck)

FILTHY BILLY puts several cigarettes on the boulder.

BETH

What're you doing?

FILTHY BILLY

Granny says he smoked.

BETH stands with FILTHY BILLY in silence for a moment. NORA's bells jingle quietly. BETH and FILTHY BILLY turn to see NORA, watching them from a distance.

FILTHY BILLY

I'm going to go in and get some grub.

BETH

Okay. I'll see you later.

BETH crosses to NORA. NORA sits on a tree stump holding her knife. She has cut herself. A rivulet of blood drips from her arm onto the snow. NORA doesn't look up.

NORA

Pretty, isn't it?

BETH

Stop that!

NORA

It's so red. (*sucking the blood from the cut on her arm*) So salty.
You'd think you were drinking the ocean.

BETH

Stop. You're making me sick.

> *NORA looks up. She has been crying. Her lips are smeared
> with the blood from her arm. She licks them clean.*

BETH

Why'd you leave?

> *NORA shrugs and wipes the blood from her hands with
> some snow.*

NORA

I've got something for you.

> *NORA reaches into her pocket and pulls out a string of
> bells just long enough for a bracelet. She drops it into
> BETH's hands.*

NORA

You like it?

BETH

I love it!

NORA

You like it better than Filthy Billy's present?

BETH

It's beautiful. I'll wear it always.

> *NORA ties the bracelet on BETH's arm. BETH shakes it.*
> *The tinkling notes bound off the trees. A few birds twitter*
> *in response.*

BETH

You'll hear me coming and going.

NORA

I'll keep track of you.

BETH

Why don't you come back?

NORA

Nah. Too crowded.

> *BETH touches NORA's face and tries to kiss her. NORA pulls*
> *back. BETH turns to go.*

NORA

Wait.

> *NORA pushes BETH up against a tree and kisses her with all*
> *of her body. Then she stops.*

NORA

You want to leave? We could leave. Today.

BETH

I can't go. What would my mother think?

NORA

You're old enough to decide for yourself. We'll go to
Vancouver. We'll say we're sisters.

> BETH laughs.

NORA

(*angrily*) You don't love me.

BETH

Sure I do.

NORA

I watch you with Dennis, and now Billy. I see how you are.

BETH

Stop watching me all the time!

NORA

You go walking in the bush, and there's lots of things watching. You want privacy, stay home.

> NORA slams the knife she's holding into the tree stump,
> then turns and runs before BETH can say anything. BETH
> watches NORA go, then pulls NORA's knife out of the stump
> and heads home.

SCENE 7

Snow falls. Time has passed. The Christmas decorations are gone.

Night. BETH sits on her porch with LUCIFER. Eventually, she hears the sound of bells quietly tinkling – NORA. She follows the sound into the barn. BETH discovers NORA and DENNIS. NORA's shirt is open, DENNIS's face is buried in her neck, his hips move against her. NORA's eyes are closed, but she opens them to see BETH watching. BETH gasps. DENNIS hears BETH and stops. He moves away from NORA, fumbling to do up his pants.

BETH
Dennis?

DENNIS
Beth, I, I ...

NORA makes eye contact with BETH, buttons her shirt, and then turns and walks into the night. BETH runs away in the opposite direction, and DENNIS chases her.

DENNIS
Beth, wait!

BETH stops, but keeps her distance from DENNIS.

DENNIS
I'm sorry. Really. I thought you weren't interested no more. I mean I never got a minute alone with you.

BETH

She's family.

DENNIS

She's a cousin. Cousins marry.

BETH

You going to marry her?

DENNIS

No, no. She wanted to go someplace. I said I would help.

BETH

If she messed around with you.

DENNIS

If she and I was friends.

BETH

Friends?

DENNIS

You don't have to live here. There's other places. Nora says
you're talking about leaving. I'm leaving. I've been making
plans. I've been saving money.

BETH

If you go, how are we going to run the farm?

DENNIS

I promised Granny I'd stick around until your father gets
out of that place, and I will. But we don't have to be around
when he gets home. We can get out of here, for good. We
could be friends.

BETH

"Friends"! Just leave me alone!

DENNIS laughs.

DENNIS

It's not me you want, anyway. You're hot for Filthy Billy.
I seen you two.

BETH

That's not true.

DENNIS

Who knew you'd fall for the mongoloid? (*laughing and
imitating Billy, mocking a proposal*) "Oh Beth (shit), will you
(fuck, damn), marry (shit, fuck, shit) me?"

*BETH slaps DENNIS. DENNIS's face darkens. He moves in
on BETH.*

DENNIS

That wasn't very nice.

BETH smells his breath now that he's closer.

BETH

You're drunk.

DENNIS

I buy you things, I treat you all nice like my girlfriend, and
that's what I get? You're a tease. You're giving it to Billy for
free, and I'm getting nothing.

BETH

I'm not giving anything to Billy.

DENNIS

Maybe I'll just pack my bags and head off now. Leave you and your mother to fend for yourselves.

BETH

Maybe I'll let your granny know about you and Nora. She'll be so pleased. Cousins marry, after all.

Tense beat.

DENNIS

We're done, you and me.

BETH

Fine by me.

DENNIS

I'm gone.

DENNIS leaves. BETH closes her eyes and begins to cry. When she opens them again, CRAZY JACK is very close, crouched down at the edge of the bush, watching her. His hair is plastered to his head, a line of spittle runs down his chin, and his shirt is wet with perspiration.

BETH

Hi. You surprised me. (*becoming anxious*) Are you okay?

CRAZY JACK runs at BETH and grabs her. She screams and tries to run, but CRAZY JACK throws her in the snow. Suddenly he twists, bats the air, and screams. The scream becomes a howl. He drops to all fours and cowers away from BETH. He bristles and growls. BETH slowly stands and claps her hands, as one would to scare off a wild animal.

BETH

Shoo! Get out of here!

CRAZY JACK retreats. He stands at a distance.

BETH

Get away! Get the hell out of here!

BETH grabs NORA's knife from her pocket and points it at CRAZY JACK.

BETH

You stay away from me. So help me God, I'll kill you.

CRAZY JACK holds out his hands in protection and looks at BETH.

CRAZY JACK

You have no idea. I try to stop it. I try to keep it to myself.

BETH lowers the knife a little.

BETH

Billy says you've got some ghost thing riding you. I didn't believe it before. But I don't want any part of it. You understand me? You quit following me. You stay away. You tried to burn down our farm! My father's gone. Dennis is gone. You ruined everything!

CRAZY JACK covers his face with both hands and sobs. His shoulders heave and he cries out. BETH backs out, still pointing the knife at him.

BETH

Stay away. Just stay away!

BETH throws the knife in the snow and runs home.
Eventually CRAZY JACK looks up in the direction BETH
went. She's gone. CRAZY JACK is still for a moment, then
he picks up the knife. He considers the knife, then holds it
high in the air and brings it down sharply toward his chest.
A howl rings through the night, followed by the flapping of
hundreds of BIRDS' wings.

. . . .

SCENE 8

The sound of birds transforms into the sound of church bells.
FILTHY BILLY works in the yard. BETH enters the yard
wearing black funeral attire.

FILTHY BILLY
How was the funeral?

BETH doesn't respond.

FILTHY BILLY
It's not your fault.

BETH
I gave him the knife.

FILTHY BILLY
Don't go blaming yourself. He's been crazy for a long time.

Beat.

BETH

They buried him right beside Sarah Kemp. That doesn't seem right. (*pause*) It was just me and Mum and the Swede. I sorta expected more people would come. I thought everyone knew Crazy Jack. (*pause*) Do you think it was that Coyote thing?

FILTHY BILLY

If it was Coyote, I think he's gone now. I don't smell him anymore. The tics and scratching are gone, and I ain't swearing anymore (shit).

FILTHY BILLY smiles. BETH laughs.

FILTHY BILLY

And I ain't swearing *much* anymore.

The two stand in silence for a moment.

FILTHY BILLY

Dennis is gone. He's going to hop a freight to Vernon. Join up.

BETH

Did Nora go with him?

FILTHY BILLY nods his head toward a figure approaching from the distance. It's NORA, carrying a carpet bag stuffed to overflowing. FILTHY BILLY smiles at BETH and heads off in the opposite direction. NORA sees BETH, and for a moment it looks like she might dart into the bushes to avoid her, but NORA keeps walking toward BETH.

BETH

Where are you going?

NORA

Does it matter?

BETH

It matters.

> *NORA pushes back the sleeves of her jacket and shows BETH*
> *that she has cut herself again. Blood drips onto the ground.*

NORA

This place is going to kill me. Nothing here but this.

BETH

Where you going to go?

NORA

I'll see which train I can get on. I got a little money from my
uncles.

BETH

They know about it?

NORA

They know they've got empty wallets.

BETH

You went after Dennis, didn't you?

NORA

That's crap!

BETH

You knew he liked me. You were jealous.

NORA

I got nothing to be jealous about. You're just some girl.
I don't need you. Plenty of boys after me.

BETH

Fine.

NORA

Fine.

> *They both cross their arms. When BETH realizes they both
> have their arms crossed, she moves her hands to her lap
> instead. Finally, she says —*

BETH

You like him better than me?

NORA

He smells like a goat. They all smell like goats. (*pause*)
What're you staying here for? Your father's coming back.
You know he is.

BETH

It's home. I don't know anything else.

NORA

You're never going to if you don't step out.

BETH

I got things to do here first. Mum needs me now. You'll
write?

NORA

Sure, I'll write. I'll find a place. Then maybe you can come.

BETH

Maybe.

>*NORA touches BETH's hair and runs her hand down BETH's face. NORA turns and begins down the road. She waves once. Spots of blood drip from her arm, leaving a trail. BETH watches NORA go and, as she does, LUCIFER wanders up to BETH and begins to rub against her leg. BETH picks LUCIFER up.*

BETH

(*to LUCIFER*) She's gone.

. . . .

SCENE 9

>*Winter turns to spring. The snow disappears, revealing the green below. The FAWN emerges and drinks from the creek. The BIRDS fly in and land on the laundry line.*

>*BETH sits in the kitchen. She is assembling her own scrapbook.*

>*FILTHY BILLY enters.*

FILTHY BILLY

Happy birthday!

>*FILTHY BILLY hands BETH a small, foil-wrapped package. She opens it.*

BETH

Chocolate! It's been so long. Where did you – ?

FILTHY BILLY

(*smiling*) Been saving up.

BETH

Thank you.

> *BETH breaks the square of chocolate in half and gives a portion to FILTHY BILLY. They eat together, luxuriating in the flavour.*

FILTHY BILLY

Beautiful day. Feels good. Spring.

BETH

Spring looks good on you, Billy.

FILTHY BILLY

(*smiling*) "Billy." I like that no one calls me "Filthy" anymore. How about you beg off going to church with your mother Sunday? You and me, we'll pack a picnic, hike up over the mountain, for your birthday.

BETH

I'd like that. I'll make a pound cake.

FILTHY BILLY

(*looking at BETH and smiling*) Sixteen looks good on you.

> *FILTHY BILLY notices BETH's scrapbook.*

FILTHY BILLY

Whatcha working on?

BETH

A scrapbook. For me.

FILTHY BILLY

Like your mum's.

BETH

Nah, mine's going to be a book of words, my words. I figure
my mum doesn't put words in her scrapbook because she
talks them all to her mother. If you can get things out of
yourself – say 'em or paste 'em into a scrapbook – then you
can sort things out.

FILTHY BILLY smiles.

*The sound of the democrat approaches the house. BETH looks
to the door, expectantly, then back to FILTHY BILLY.*

BETH

He's here.

FILTHY BILLY

You ready?

BETH shrugs. She's not sure.

BETH

House is clean. (*grabbing a tray of oatcakes from the counter*)
And I baked his favourite oatcakes.

FILTHY BILLY

It'll be fine. (*making eye contact*) And I'll be here.

*FILTHY BILLY squeezes BETH's hand and exits to the
yard. BETH tucks the scrapbook away and braces herself for
the unknown. MOTHER enters.*

MOTHER

(*to BETH*) Move slowly, talk quietly. Don't expect much.

> *FILTHY BILLY helps FATHER into the house. FATHER wears the same clothes he wore the night of the fire.*

MOTHER

We're home, John.

> *BETH looks at FATHER. There is recognition on his face for a moment, then he stares at his feet. He is pale and tired and weak.*

MOTHER

Let's get you into your chair.

> *They sit him down in his chair in the living room. BETH puts FATHER's favourite Caruso record on the gramophone.*

MOTHER

Do me a favour, Billy. Talk to John. You have a way with him. Tell him about that tractor we're looking to buy. And the cow you had to shoot last month. It was one of his favourites.

FILTHY BILLY

Sure thing, ma'am.

MOTHER

Hopefully he says something to you. I get more response from my mother.

> *MOTHER exits to her bedroom. FILTHY BILLY whispers in FATHER's ear as BETH watches. FATHER responds in a quiet voice.*

FATHER

We were late planting last year. Then that storm nearly wiped us out. I don't want that happening again.

FILTHY BILLY

We'll be on it. It's going to be a good year. I can feel it.

FILTHY BILLY heads out to the field. MOTHER brings FATHER a pillow and blanket.

MOTHER

Comfortable, John?

FATHER nods.

MOTHER

I'll see if I can find something to help.

BETH brings FATHER the tray of oatcakes. He slowly takes one and has a bite. MOTHER pages through her scrapbook. BETH looks on anxiously.

BETH

Anything?

MOTHER

(*shaking her head, then lightly gesturing to the page*) If he had been hit by lightning, then I could help ...

MOTHER and BETH exchange a small smile. MOTHER returns to the scrapbook.

....

SCENE 10

Three days later. FATHER remains in the chair listening to the same Caruso record, staring at the wall. BETH is in the kitchen working on her scrapbook. The record ends. FATHER moans.

BETH

Dad, do you want something to eat?

No response.

BETH

Do you want me to put the Caruso record on again? How about we listen to something else? You've been listening to it for three days straight.

FATHER shakes his head.

BETH

More Caruso? Okay.

BETH walks to the gramophone. As she lifts the needle to replay the record, FATHER runs his hand up the back of BETH's leg, under her skirt. BETH spins around and steps back, pointing directly into FATHER's face.

BETH

You never touch me again. Keep your goddamned hands off me. You're my father, for Christ's sake.

BETH holds her ground and keeps her eyes on FATHER. He begins to cry, hard. BETH is surprised. She puts her hand on his shoulder. He sobs harder. She offers him some of the oatcakes, but he sobs and knocks the oatcakes out of her hand. At her wits' end, BETH slaps him across the face.

BETH

Enough of this foolishness. Quit acting like a child.

FATHER holds his cheek and stops crying. MOTHER enters and sees the oatcakes on the ground.

MOTHER

What's the matter?

BETH

(*throwing up her hands*) I don't know.

MOTHER approaches FATHER. She touches him on the shoulder gently.

MOTHER

John? Are you all right?

FATHER pulls away, retreating inside himself. MOTHER sighs. BETH watches as MOTHER picks up the oatcakes and brings them into the kitchen. MOTHER stares up to the heavens, as if she's hoping her dead mother will give her a solution. BETH makes a decision. She places her scrapbook in front of her mother.

MOTHER

What's this?

BETH

A scrapbook. My scrapbook. I made it.

MOTHER looks to BETH, surprised.

MOTHER

Well I'll be …

> *MOTHER opens BETH's scrapbook and looks at its blank, new pages. MOTHER opens her own scrapbook and flips through to find the page she is looking for. Carefully she removes the butterfly from its page and affixes it to the first page of BETH's scrapbook.*

MOTHER

The butterfly. To get you started.

> *A shared moment between MOTHER and daughter. Then both women look to FATHER, who continues to sit in his chair, withdrawn. Finally, BETH decides she needs to take action.*

BETH

He can't just sit in that chair for the rest of his life. He needs some air. Help me get him up. Let's get him into the democrat for a ride.

> *BETH and MOTHER help FATHER stand.*

BETH

Come on, Dad, we're going outside.

> *BETH and MOTHER walk FATHER outside and help him into the democrat. FILTHY BILLY jumps onto the democrat with them. MOTHER drives along Blood Road. Up ahead, the road swarms with TURTLES. BETH points toward the TURTLES.*

BETH

The turtles are back!

MOTHER stops the cart. The TURTLES cross in such numbers that there seems to be a moving, living blanket crossing the road.

BETH
  Come on, Billy.

FILTHY BILLY and BETH jump down from the democrat and start helping TURTLES up to the red sand bank where they will lay their eggs. Music plays. BETH and FILTHY BILLY chat happily. FILTHY BILLY picks up a turtle and turns it the wrong direction. It rights itself. FILTHY BILLY and BETH laugh. It's a simple, good moment.

MOTHER climbs down from the democrat and helps FATHER down.

BETH's bracelet jingles on her arm. She looks at the bracelet, taking in the sound. She stares down the road.

FILTHY BILLY stands behind BETH, holding her shoulders.

BETH turns and looks at her mother and father for a moment, then turns her attention back to the road. BETH, FILTHY BILLY, MOTHER, and FATHER all stand in the middle of Blood Road and watch the TURTLES.

End of play.

ACKNOWLEDGMENTS

Many thanks to all of the people and organizations that supported the development of this script: its original production company, Western Canada Theatre; Laurel Green, Vicki Stroich, and Vanessa Porteous at Alberta Theatre Projects in Calgary; Lori Marchand, Kevin Loring, Heather Cant, and Holly Lewis for their dramaturgical guidance; the many actors who participated in readings and workshops at both ATP and WCT; Cory Sincennes for his design guidance; and Braden Griffiths for his ingenuity with puppets and for being involved in every step of the development of this project.

My deepest gratitude to Gail Anderson-Dargatz. Thank you for trusting me with your story.

ABOUT THE PLAYWRIGHT

Daryl Cloran is the Artistic Director of the Citadel Theatre in Edmonton, Alberta. He moved to Edmonton from Kamloops, British Columbia, where he served as Artistic Director of Western Canada Theatre for six seasons.

Cloran's directing credits include *Shakespeare in Love* (Citadel Theatre/Royal Manitoba Theatre Centre), *Love's Labour's Lost* (Bard on the Beach), *Liberation Days* (Theatre Calgary/Western Canada Theatre), *Mary Poppins* (WCT/Persephone), *Tribes* (Canadian Stage/Theatrefront/Theatre Aquarius), *And All For Love* (National Arts Centre), *Generous* (Tarragon), and *Afterplay* (Shaw Festival). Cloran was also the Founding Artistic Director of Theatrefront in Toronto, where he directed numerous international collaborations, including *Return (The Sarajevo Project)*, produced in Bosnia and Toronto; and *Ubuntu (The Cape Town Project)*, produced in South Africa, Halifax, Toronto, Calgary, Edmonton, and Vancouver.

Cloran's work has been nominated for Dora Awards (Toronto), Betty Awards (Calgary), Saskatoon and Area Theatre Awards, Jessie Awards (Vancouver), and Ovation Awards (Vancouver). He has been awarded the Canada Council's John Hirsch Prize for Outstanding Emerging Theatre Director, the Toronto Theatre Emerging Artist Award, and a Robert Merritt Award for Outstanding Director (Halifax).

Cloran lives in Edmonton with his wife Holly Lewis and their two sons Liam and Jack.